AS FAR AS
FAR ENOUGH

Claire Rooney

Bella
BOOKS
2008

Bella Books, Inc.
P.O. Box 10543
Tallahassee, FL 32302

Printed in the United States of America on acid-free paper
First Edition

Editor: Cindy Cresap
Cover designer: LA Callaghan

ISBN-10: 1-59493-140-2
ISBN-13: 978-1-59493-140-6

To
Darlin' Neal,
who took the shifting sands and gave me something better to stand on

Acknowledgments
No woman is an island, though some of us try really hard.

A special thank you to:

David Bernstein for listening even when he didn't think I thought he was

Laurie Kutchins for being brave enough to answer the hard questions honestly

Mary Thompson for the enlightening arguments over obscure points of narrative theory

Susan Facknitz for giving me the ability to decipher Emily's horrible handwriting

Inman Majors for the funny parts

Cindy Tingen for being there every Saturday at 8:30 without fail

The Gaston Group for the pumpkin goo and other squishy stuff

The Taos Summer Writer's Conference for their support and encouragement

Kate for helping me explore the issues

And to Dorothy for the wicked dreams

A very special acknowledgment:
And not least, my heartfelt thanks to the extraordinary woman who suggested (oh, so politely) that if I didn't like her book, I should go write my own. Wow! What a great idea!

About the Author

Claire Rooney lives on the east coast and divides her time between the mountains and the sea. During the day, she moonlights as an Analyst, holding a degree in Computer Science with a minor in Creative Writing. At night, she comes home to an ever revolving number of critters and works hard until the wee hours writing and trying to keep cat paws off the keyboard. Claire has been a frequent collaborator and contributor to Sister Speak, a literary journal and was the guest editor in 2007. She is, at this time, far enough over forty for it to be rude for you to ask and 100% certain that gravity works. But she's still cute as a button. Look for her next book, *The Color of Dust*, coming soon in 2009.

Chapter One: BRIDGES

On my wedding day, while my father was putting on his tuxedo, I was pulling on a pair of black leather pants. As I shimmied the leather over my thighs, I pictured him tying on his bow tie, his long, nimble fingers making quick, precise pulls. While I buckled, zippered and buttoned, I imagined him sliding the jacket up over his still-broad shoulders, pulling down on his shirt cuffs with short, sharp tugs. I pulled my tank top over my head and imagined him standing in front of his mirror, looking himself over with a critical eye, lifting a hand to smooth back his steel gray hair. Flashes of brilliance would sparkle from his diamond cufflinks. He would tuck a small white rose into his lapel with a warm glimmer of gold gleaming from his wristwatch. I pictured him stepping into his shiny black shoes, toes pointed like a dancer's, bending to arrange the tassels. I shoved my feet into a shiny new pair of Rockstomper boots and buckled them tight against my calves.

I stood in the middle of my room . . . but maybe I shouldn't say my room. It was the same room that had been wrapped around me ever since I was a child, but I never felt any sense of affinity with it. Mostly, I think, because I never had any say about what went inside it, not the color of the carpet, not the pictures on the wall, not the toys in toy chest, not the clothes in the closet. My life had been full of the lack of choices. Even through the pallid rebellions of my teenaged years, all my choices were made for me, what I would eat, who my friends were, the shade of my pantyhose. This room, my life, never had a chance to be my own. And then, the last straw fell, the one where I couldn't do enough pretending to make it go away but wasn't strong enough to see it through. I had come to a point where I had to make a choice or give up choosing forever. At twenty-four, the point seemed a long time in coming.

I stood in the middle of this room holding myself still, listening for my father's heavy tread on the circular stair, for the tiny clicking of my mother's heels on the marble in the foyer, the whoosh of the front doors opening. But there was nothing to hear, just the awkward beating of my heart and the soft squeak of my boots as I shifted my weight from foot to foot. The house was too big, the front hall miles away, too far for me to hear the sharp bark of my father's voice or to see the timid dip of my mother's head, the slight hunching of her shoulders as his hand reached out for her. The silence howled against my ears. It always did in this house, this cavern of stucco, stone and ivy.

The new leather of my pants creaked and moaned as I walked over to the window and drew back a corner of the heavy curtain. I squinted my eyes against the bright sunshine and watched my parents walk down the portico steps, my mother, tottering on her heels, my father's hand wrapped firmly around her elbow, his long fingers denting the flesh of her arm. They ducked into the limousine that was sitting patiently in the circular drive. It seemed to me that limos were always waiting much more than they were going. I always felt sorry for the drivers lounging around in their black suits inside a black car with the sun shining.

A second limo sat parked in the drive, a white one. Jeffries leaned against the driver's side door, his legs crossed at the ankles, smoke from his cigarette curling up from his fingers. He was a good driver, as far as drivers went, always polite and never judgmental in that silently sneering way that some of them had if they disapproved of the destination or the company they kept. I'd always liked Jeffries. I was sorry my father picked him to drive me to the church. He blew out a thin stream of blue smoke from tightly pursed lips. With a flick of his wrist, he looked at his watch.

There was only one small hour left standing between now and the time that I should be getting into that car. He was waiting patiently in his black suit standing in the bright sun. What a shame it was that he would die of heat prostration or lung cancer long before he would see me tiptoeing down the stairs in my wedding gown. The dress still lay draped over the foot of my bed, like an abandoned lover, still wrapped in its plastic sheathing. I watched Jeffries wave a lazy arm in the air as the black limo drove away. It circled around the drive and disappeared behind the long line of hedges that hid the less fortunate parts of the world from our more privileged eyes, all the honest dirt and toil carefully hidden behind a veil of green leaves and red blossoms. I let the curtain fall into place and turned to face the interior gloom.

The room was quiet and still with only the faint whir of the air conditioner humming just at the edge of hearing. This room was always too quiet. Even when I was a little girl, sounds crashed against the oak paneled walls and fell in shattered bits to drown inside the deep pile of plush carpeting. When I was very small, I used to scream sometimes just so I could hear something, a faint vibration, the glimmer of an echo, the sound of the nanny's feet thudding down the hallway. I wanted to scream now, a deep, ragged, epic scream, large and long enough to shatter the silence of all those years, but I didn't dare. I paid the staff an obscene amount of money, a significant chunk of my carefully hoarded allowance, to stay out of this wing. And they would, but not if I started screaming, not if they thought I was hurt.

In a way, it was money needlessly spent. I didn't need to pay them. They would have honored my wish even if I'd just asked for the time to be alone in my last hours of singleness. They understood what it was to be bound into servitude. Their bindings were born of necessity instead of political expedience, but it was still the same chain. They were good people. That thought came with only a bit of a twinge. God only knows how many rules I was breaking just thinking that, thinking of the staff as real people. But they were, and I wanted to leave them with something for the trouble I would be causing. In just a few hours, their lives would become a frantic kind of hell. I counted to ten to steady myself and then crept out of the room, tiptoeing over the plush carpet, quieter than a mouse, quieter than the maids, in search of a pair of scissors.

I started with my bangs. A deep breath, a quick snip, and twelve inches of shiny black hair lay in a frayed rope on the bathroom floor. Small spikes stuck up from my forehead. That was it, then. The first bridge was burning and I could almost smell the smoke. I wiped the sweat off my palms, got a firm grip on the kitchen shears and snipped again and again and again.

The strands fell to the floor in chunks that seemed heavier than they should have been. I imagined my father, as the scissors snicked, riding in the backseat of the limo. His face would be serene as he counted the cost of every hors d'oeuvre, every bouquet, every bowl of punch, and weighed them against his gains. Those gains included, of course, the son-in-law he purchased, the young man with the old money ties who would give him entrée into new conduits of power, buy him things his newly minted money could never touch. A daughter was not so high a price for that, and the net balance would be to his advantage. It always was. Of my mother, I pictured very little. I could see her long

4

dark hair, pale skin and quiet gray eyes. She would be sitting in silence, small and frail, shivering slightly under the cold shadow of my father's indomitable will.

A shade of her face stared out at me from the mirror. My coloring I got from her, the blue-black hair and pasty-skinned paleness, but the square jaw and the height came from my father. I stood just an inch and a half shy of six feet. My eyes came from him, too. They were brown like his, like a fine dark chocolate, like rich garden soil. Like horseshit.

One last snip of the shears and my hair lay curled on the floor all around me, dark strands on the cold white marble, a full circle of burned bridges, the blackened remains of all I ever knew. A sense of loss swelled inside me, filling my throat, stealing my breath. It was not the loss of the things I would be leaving behind or for the things I wouldn't own anymore, but for all the things that never were mine and never would be now. The scissors fell from my hand and hit the marble with a clatter.

I pulled myself together, blew my nose, dried my eyes and swept my hair off the floor. I stood over the commode and watched it swirl around and around, flushing five times before it finally all disappeared. The kitchen shears, I tucked into my back pocket as I shut the bathroom door behind me. Standing in the darkest corner of my closet, I began to pack a pile of bright new blue jeans and crisp white T-shirts into a set of motorcycle saddlebags, settling them over top of my silk underwear and lace filigree bras. The clothes went into one side and the money went into the other, tightly bundled in thousand dollar stacks.

This plan had been a while in the making, ever since my father first introduced me to my new fiancée, and I was sure I had it all figured out. There were maps in the side pockets of the saddle bags with eight possible routes marked out in yellow, gas stations dotted in red. I had phone numbers for all the smallest motel chains and a prepaid cell phone tucked inside the money bag.

It was just starting into March. Balmy in southern California, the beginning of spring and beautiful riding weather. I'd been to Paris once, in the springtime, and summered twice in the Swiss Alps. I spent most of my falls at the house my father kept in Washington, D.C., where fur coats hung in the hall closet. But for all of that, I lived my life in southern California and had no real concept of weather. The sun shone or the wind blew. It rained on occasion, and maybe there was hail on a special day. Sometimes the earth moved, but that was all I knew. It never occurred to me to pack a sweater.

I buckled the bags closed and thought of the guests waiting at the church. The haute monde swathed in the best haute couture, not for my sake, or even for my father's, but for the hope of being seen, for the dream of being filmed or photographed wearing the right thing, standing beside the right person. The peacocks preening for the vultures. I could imagine them growing ever more impatient, shifting in their places as delicate bottoms became bruised by the hard pews. They would murmur polite questions to their neighbors that would grow less polite over time.

I didn't have time to feel sorry for them, only about ten minutes left before Jeffries would start to wonder, fifteen before the search began. I slipped on my black leather jacket, threw the saddlebags across my shoulder and slipped out of the house through the service door. I made my way through the garden paths to the groundskeeper's garage where, even in the dust and dim light, my motorcycle sat gleaming. A beacon of truth in my life full of lies. I strapped down the saddlebags, wriggled my fingers into my gloves and threw a leg over.

An hour later, I was standing at the top of a tall bridge, the bike grumbling quietly to itself leaning over on its kickstand in the emergency lane. Warm sunshine caressed the shoulders of my jacket while a stiff breeze off the bay combed through my ragged two inches of hair. I clutched at my cell phone, the fancy one my father gave me with caller ID, a camera, video streaming and a GPS tracking device he didn't think I knew about. I stared at the blank screen. By this time, he would be talking softly, urgently, with the seething groom at the end of the long aisle, issuing instructions to his toadies or trying to bully the police into organizing a search party. Being a man of means, it would take him a while to think of the simple solution. I thought of the passing minutes as small drops of water dripping off the outstretched wings of the sculpted ice swan.

On the bridge, cars and trucks streamed past, sometimes honking, sometimes shouting, mostly oblivious. I leaned against the railing and watched the afternoon sun glitter off the water far below me, at the tiny whitecapped waves and toy boats with their colorful sails. We had sailed under this bridge, my father and I, countless times when I was small and still too young to understand the art of the deal, that one hand gives while the other hand takes, that to profit you have to spend, or that image is everything, nothing is for free and everyone is expendable. The bright sparkles of sunshine stung my eyes. I swiped at them with the heel of my hand.

The phone chirped and made me jump. I almost couldn't believe the number on the screen. It was not my father's number. It was Weasel's, my father's secretary. My fist spasmed around the phone. I would have crushed it if I could, ground it into dust, scattered its atoms to the wind. The flame of rage burned through me and turned my doubts to ash, blurring my world before spilling it down my cheeks. I screamed then, there on the bridge, where no one cared to hear me. It was long and loud and epic. I threw the phone as far out over the water as I could. I didn't stay to watch it splash. My bike roared to life with an impatient growl, the back tire screeching as I twisted hard on the throttle, blazing a short score of rubber, burning the last bridge behind me.

Chapter Two: WRECKAGE

Nineteen days of stretched out highways, through big cities and small towns, over tall mountains and flatlands, wide rivers and rolling green foothills. It ended on a thin dark line of a rural East Coast road with a pair of glowing eyes ahead of me, the sheen of a recent rain on the pavement, the asphalt twisting wildly underneath a canopy of overhanging trees. I remember swerving to miss the deer as he tried to leap over me, the back tire of my motorcycle screeching and skidding as a hoof flew in toward my faceplate.

Lying in a culvert, cold water seeping through my leathers, warm liquid pooling against my cheek, I was thinking that I should take my helmet off before I drowned. I blinked and was standing in a field of knee-high wildflowers, their gently swaying petals gray in the moonlight. A chill breeze rustled through the field. The flowers shivered and bobbed their heads. I shivered too, my head throbbing as the breeze ruffled through my hair and nipped at my ears. I raised my hands and touched them to my face. My cheek was damp, my fingers sticky. The stars wheeled overhead, the moon rose higher in the sky and started to set. A pinpoint of light caught my eye, shimmering in the distance. There was something special about that light. Something I should remember.

"Oh," I said speaking softly to the flowers. "I'm supposed to go to the light."

There was no one there to stop me, so I moved toward the light as best I could with the ground rolling and heaving under my feet.

It was a halogen light, bright and blue. Seemed odd to me, though, that the entrance to heaven should be lit with a halogen light. I tried to frown, but the muscles in my face wouldn't work. Underneath the light was a door. Stranger still. I thought heaven was supposed to have a pearly gate, not one made of pine and in the shape of a barn door, but then, there were a lot of things I didn't know about heaven. Maybe this was the back-door and the only way in for people like me. I knocked softly, but God, I supposed, had pretty good hearing.

"Can I come in?" I whispered into the pine. There was a sound of movement inside, a shuffling of feet and a wet sounding snuffle, but the door stayed closed. I puffed a tight little chuff that was almost a sob and slumped against the wood. The door slid a little to the side, and then I remembered, *God helps them who help themselves.* I leaned a little harder, and the door slid open.

It was dark inside and smelled of horses and hay, but it was warmer than outside and I was cold and wet. I closed the door behind me, staggered over to a corner piled with loose hay and slid down the wall. Sitting in the hay, I hugged my knees tight against my chest. There was a snort above me, and something snuffed at my hair. I heard stamping and then another sound, a soft, concerned nickering. A blanket fell over me. A smelly, coarse blanket, but its rough warmth was welcome. I snuggled deep into the hay, pulled the blanket over my head and went to sleep.

· · ·

"Good morning, everyone!" said a bright, cheery voice.

It was the kind of voice that I've always hated, coming from people full of false hopes and hidden agendas. I stirred a little under the blanket and tried to open my eyes, but they were too heavy.

"Hey, Sergeant, look what I have for you!"

There was an excited whinnying above me, the sound of crunching and the smell of pulped apples.

"Sergeant," the voice said with sudden impatience. It was a candid tone, truly unhappy, sincerely irritated. I liked it a lot better. "Honestly, boy. Why do you keep throwing your blanket on the ground?"

Brisk morning air hit my face, sunlight stabbed red through my eyelids. There was a long silence, then the twittering of a far-off bird, the nearby screech of a blue jay. Wood creaked above me, and Sergeant huffed apple breath into my hair. I tried to say something, but it came out as a groan.

"Oh, my god." I heard her whisper. Feet went crunching through the hay. A faucet ran from somewhere, and I heard the feet return. A cold, damp cloth swiped gently at my cheeks and eyes. I cracked my eyes open to see a thin-faced woman leaning over me, a dark-stained rag dangling from her fingers.

"Ouch," I said.

"Are you all right?" the woman asked then shook her head. "No, course, you're not. Don't move, okay? I'm going to call an ambulance."

"No!" I reached out and grabbed her wrist, grasping it with shaky fingers. "Please don't call anybody." I struggled to sit, yanking awkwardly on her arm until she slipped a hand under my shoulder and set me upright against the wall. I leaned against the wood blinking hard, trying to see past the funny black spots hopping around in front of my eyes.

"But you're hurt," she said, scooting back a bit.

"I think I bumped my head," I told her waving a hand in front of my face to shoo the spots away. "Please, just let me sit here for a minute. I'm sure I'll be fine."

She looked at me doubtfully. "It's not just a bump, lady. You have huge gash on your forehead."

"Lady?" For a moment, I wondered if I had worn the wrong clothes. Maybe I was sitting in a pile of hay on the floor of some stranger's barn in a cocktail dress. But, no, I remembered, I hadn't packed any dresses. I looked down at myself, still wrapped in scuffed muddy leather, minus a big chunk from my left knee where the skin underneath was raw and red. I ran my fingers through my hair, still short and spiky, and waggled my feet, watching the scraped toes of my boots sway back and forth. At least everything moved. I scratched gently at an itchy patch of dried crust on my cheek and looked at my fingernails at flakes of old blood and dirt.

"If you don't get that stitched, you'll have a really bad scar," she was saying.

I thought that she might have said something before that, too, and I wondered what I missed, but it was hard to concentrate on her words when there was such a sing-songy lilt to her voice. She talked funny, too, like there were too many vowels in her words.

I blinked at her. "I'm sorry, what were you saying?"

She frowned and dabbed at my cheek with her rag. "Your head, you need to get it patched, or you're going to have a scar."

I raised a hand to my eyebrow and prodded gingerly. It felt like it was much larger than it should have been, and it hurt. In fact, the whole left side of my face hurt. I thought about it for a second and decided that my entire left side hurt, so I shrugged my right shoulder instead. "What's one more scar?"

The woman sat back on her heels, hands dangling loosely between her knees, looking at me curiously, like maybe she was wondering where else I had scars on my body and just how I got them there. I wasn't talking about those kinds of scars, but it seemed too complicated to explain, and I was too busy staring

11

at her. Her face was almost familiar, not like I knew her from somewhere, but like I'd seen her look before and it meant something good. Something about her felt very comfortable to me or, at least, non-threatening. Maybe it was the way she was dressed in her faded blue-jean jacket, white-button down shirt and old cowboy boots. She had a really bad haircut and pale squinting eyes that made her look like a female version of a young John Wayne. Much prettier, though.

"Listen," I said, "can you help me? I need to find my bike and get it off the road before someone sees it." That wasn't quite what I meant to say, but I wasn't thinking clearly. My head felt a little lopsided, and the world seemed more monochrome than it should have been. "I mean, I wouldn't want anyone to run over it. I don't think it's very far from here."

She jerked her chin at me. "Your head got a pretty good whack, there, hon. I don't think it's a good idea for you to be lifting anything heavy right now, and you definitely shouldn't be riding."

"The bike's not very heavy. Please. It's all I have. Everything I own is inside the saddlebags." I thought about the money, my driver's license with my real name on it, and the two pairs of clean underwear that I still had left and would just hate to lose. Everything else in there was disgusting.

"Well." She paused to study me with intense eyes. She shook her head, and her face softened a little, though the corners of her eyes didn't lose their little crinkles. "I have a trailer that I use for hauling hay. Maybe we can get your bike on that. We'll have to get the blood off your face first, though, or you'll be scaring people."

I relaxed a little. If she could joke about it then it would be all right. "Thanks." But, then again, that might not have been a joke.

She nodded and stood. She seemed very tall from where I was sitting, leggy in her blue jeans. Her blond flyaway hair, long in the back, short in the front, stirred even in the light currents drifting through the barn. She held out her hands. I stared at them, at their roughened redness, at her short round nails, at the smear of dirt in the crease of her palm. They were working hands, hard, callused, honest hands. I grabbed them, and she hauled me to my feet. I managed to stand successfully, swaying only a little with her fingers clamped firmly around my elbow. She had a strong grip and her hands were warm. When I leaned against her, she seemed a very solid woman. I let her take more of my weight, leaning harder with my arm draped across her shoulders. I blinked at her eyebrows.

"I'm taller than you," I said stupidly.

She looked at me with a slight tilt of her chin and the ghost of a smile. "Why, so you are," she said and shuffled me out of the barn.

It took a bit of shoving to get my bike onto her trailer, with her doing most of the shoving and me panting hard, trying not to faint or lose my lunch. The bike was pretty roughed up on the left side, just like I was. The paint was scraped and the tank dented, the windscreen had a crack running through it, the turn light was broken, and the mirror dangled from a thin wire, but I thought it probably looked a lot worse than it was. I wasn't much of a mechanic by any stretch of the imagination, but it didn't look like anything major was broken, nothing that I couldn't patch with a little duct tape and ingenuity.

I'd always been good at fixing things, toys, book bindings, loose buttons, jammed Mont Blancs, but it wasn't something I was encouraged to do. My father paid people to fix things for him, and my mother never seemed to realize when something was broken, but I liked to know how things worked. It seemed to me that the better you knew how something was supposed to behave, the less likely it was to surprise you, so I made a point to learn a little something about motorcycles and four-stroke engines. It was one of the only times that I disobeyed a direct order from my father, who believed that mucking about with mechanical things was not acceptable behavior for girls in general and especially not for girls like me. His rage had been an awesome thing, and I trembled to think of it.

My hands were still shaking as we drove back toward the barn in her ancient pickup truck that smelled of old leather and leaky exhaust, its blue paint faded almost to white. A jumble of crushed Coke cans rattled musically on the floorboards as the trailer bounced along behind us.

"It looks like I'll have to make a few repairs," I said with my hands folded tightly across my middle. "But nothing looks seriously broken. The mirror is a special order part, but I can tape it into place. It just needs to stay on long enough to get me . . ."

I shut my mouth. As far as I had come, that was still the biggest question. I poked my toe at a can that tumbled across my foot. To get me where? Where was far enough, or was there any such a place?

I saw her glance at me curiously, but she didn't ask. She had the funniest eyes I'd ever seen, large and round, of a hard-to-define color, a pale ice blue in the sunshine that turned a dark storm cloud gray in the shadows. I remembered the way she looked at me in the barn and found their intensity a little disturbing. I looked out the window instead.

We turned off the road onto her gravel drive, and I noticed a small sign by the entrance that I had completely missed last night in the dark. Laurelvalley B&B it said in slightly faded, nearly professional looking letters.

"Your house is a bed-and-breakfast?" I asked turning my head gently to look at her.

She sighed slightly. It was a tired sound, like the tail end of a long story. "I pretend that it is. It's a very old farmhouse, a homestead that some ancient branch of my family built in the mid eighteen hundreds. There's an interesting history to it, how it survived the Civil War and all, but, truth be told, I'm so far off the beaten path that no one ever stays here, at least, not often.

I just get the occasional artist who comes through to paint the mountains or a honeymoon couple who don't intend to leave their room anyway." She smiled at me a little sheepishly. It was a sweet smile, and it took me by surprise. It made me smile back at her, one of my rare honest smiles. She blushed and turned away. That surprised me, too.

"In the fall," she said staring over the top of the steering wheel, "people from the eastern part of the state come to see the leaves change color. They only stay the night and then they go home. It doesn't bring in much, but sometimes it's nice to have people around. All the rest of the time, this is just a regular old farm. I grow a few things now and again, and there's a good-sized apple orchard over the hill there." She waved her hand in the air in no particular direction.

I could see the house through the truck's pockmarked windshield. It sat on top of a gentle swell of earth, bright white against the soft green of the new spring grass. Its sharply peaked gables pointed red tin into the sky and the faded gray of a barn was visible a little ways behind. Soft blue shadows of mountains, still capped with the morning's mist, rose over the treetops. I could see why an artist would want to paint here. It made me wish I had a camera.

"Do you have any guests now?" I asked.

"No," she said, shaking her head. "It's still too early in the spring. The weather's nice most of the time, but it's unpredictable. We might get one day of summer temperatures and then two days later it'll be snowing. It stays chaotic all the way through until May before it finally settles into summer."

I chewed on my lower lip for a while as I counted my options. One. I shifted a little in my seat. "Do you think I could stay for a few days? Just until I fix the bike. I'm sure it won't take long, only a day or two. I can pay you something."

She turned her head to look at me with her funny colored eyes full of concern. "I still think you should go to a hospital or at least see a doctor."

I turned away from her again. "I can't."

"No insurance?"

I gave her a quick, tight smile, but I didn't say anything. I rubbed at a sore spot on the back of my neck and looked out the window, hoping she'd take my discomfort for embarrassment. My whole life had been a lie of one sort or another. I was tired of it and had no desire to begin twisting a new tangle, especially here in such a beautiful place.

"Well," she said after only a slight hesitation, "I don't see why you can't stay at least one day. You probably ought to get some rest anyhow. You're looking a little green around the gills."

I gave her a puzzled glance. "What does that mean?"

She glanced back at me unsmiling. "You look like you're going to be sick."

Of course, as soon as she said it, my stomach gave a lurch and my skin went cold and clammy. Thankfully, we'd just pulled up to the house. If we had kept moving just another hundred yards, I would have thrown up all over her Coke cans. I must have overdone it trying to help her move the bike. When I stepped out of the truck, my vision started going spotty again, and I was a little unsteady on my feet. She came around to my side, grabbed my arm and threw it around her shoulder. She wrapped her other arm around my waist and helped me climb the porch steps. The front door was unlocked and we staggered through it, into a small foyer. A quick turn to the left and we were in an old-fashioned parlor. I collapsed onto her couch, sinking into the velveteen cushions. She knelt beside me and tucked a pillow under my head, brushing a stray fringe of hair from my forehead.

"We're going to have to do something about that gash, you know," she said with a curious tilt of her head.

"Couple of Band-Aids. It'll be fine," I mumbled at her. My lips felt thick and tired. I closed my eyes and felt her hand warm against my cheek.

"Stay here, okay? I'll get the saddlebags off your bike."

I didn't want her to do that. There were too many secrets

in those bags, things that would be dangerous for her to know, buried under a thin layer of smelly socks. "Hey," I lifted my head and called out after her, but she didn't answer. My head felt too fuzzy to get up from the soft, comfortable couch, so I let it go. Maybe the socks would stop her from digging. If not, then the dirty underwear surely would.

I closed my eyes again and wondered where I was, exactly. I'd just been driving. My maps had been soaked to a pulp and then dried with the pages stuck together. The motel phone numbers were ink smeared and unreadable, or no longer in service, but that hadn't mattered. My cheap cell phone died after the first downpour I drove through, in Arizona of all places, where I nearly froze to death in the desert. After that, I just followed random signs that said east, more or less thinking that I'd eventually reach the Atlantic Ocean and then maybe I would try to get across it somehow. I had no idea how far the ocean was from here, wherever here was, exactly. I wondered about the John Wayne woman with her sharp-planed face and intense staring eyes. I wondered how she got to be here, living alone on a farm it seemed, and what kind of breakfasts she served. I was hoping for pancakes. Somehow, with all the fuzz between my ears, it never occurred to me to wonder what her name was.

She made me a ham and cheese sandwich and poured me a glass of sweet iced tea then kept me awake all day long asking inane questions about the days of the week, what year it was, the name of the president, and did I remember what color wallpaper there was in my kitchen. I didn't recall having ever been in a kitchen, so I couldn't answer that one, and I wouldn't answer any personal questions. That seemed to bother her a great deal. She kept mentioning doctors and hospitals until I rattled off the names of ninety-nine of our currently elected senators and what states they represented. I could have told her what committees they were on, the names of all their spouses and what sort of graft

17

they preferred, but I didn't want to upset her any more than I already had. I didn't want to upset myself either.

She gave in finally and put me to bed with a pair of borrowed pajamas in a smallish room with wide, chestnut floorboards. The furniture was plain but glowed with a deep patina of age and good care. She helped me into a bed with a simple knotty-pine headboard and tucked a checkered quilt up under my chin. My saddlebags sat on the cedar chest at the foot of the bed, unopened. She bathed and bandaged the road rash on my knee, tucked it under the covers and then moved higher on the bed. She sat next to me and began swabbing my forehead with cotton balls and peroxide. The cold tickling foam stung my cut, itched at my brain and kept making me want to sneeze. When she finished swabbing, she dabbed lightly with a towel and started sticking little Band-Aids on me, one after another, in a neat row of X's that ran from my temple to just over the bridge of my nose. It hurt where she had to pull on my skin to make the ends meet, but I didn't whimper too much.

"Thank you for helping me," I said, watching her rip open another Band-Aid package. She added the torn wax paper to the pile on the nightstand. "Hey, what's your name? I'm sorry I forgot to ask earlier."

"My name is Meri," she answered, carefully sticking on the last Band-Aid to the end of the long row. "Meri Donovan. That's M-E-R-I, as in happy. It's French."

"Je pense que non. Le mot est joyeux. Parlez-vous français?"

"No, I don't." She flushed slightly, unstuck a strand of my hair from underneath the edge of the last Band-Aid and combed through my bangs with her fingers. "I think that will help a little, but you're still going to have a bad scar." She lightly traced the swollen line of my eyebrow with her thumb. "You have a pretty face. It seems kind of a shame."

"Are you?" I asked.

She blinked at me with that funny little tilt to her head. "Am I what?"

18

"Are you happy, as in M-E-R-I?" It was an impulsive question. I don't know why I asked it. Her state of mind shouldn't have meant anything to me. I had no business being there at her house, and I certainly wasn't going to stay for very long, but still, I found myself hoping she would smile at me and say yes. She didn't. Her face shut down faster than a door slamming shut. She scooped the pile of Band-Aid wrappers into her hands and crumpled them into a ball.

"What's your name?" she asked.

"My friends call me Bea." That was a bit of a stretch. I didn't have any friends, and the ones that I might have had certainly wouldn't have called me Bea. It was the name I'd been using on my trek across country, when I had to have a name at all, but it was too close to a lie for my comfort, and it must have shown on my face.

Her eyes turned sharp and wary. "I have an aunt named Bea," she said. "Well, Beatrice, really. She's a little old roly-poly woman with blue hair and a wicked tongue." Her smile was almost grim. "You don't look like a Bea to me."

I felt my face flushing and her eyes narrowed a little more. The line of her mouth grew thinner making the point of her chin look almost angular. I didn't like it.

"It's just what people call me," I said. "Bea stands for the letter B, short for B.B. or Biker Babe." It was the name that the gals in the motorcycle shop christened me with, hooting and whistling, the day I showed up in my leathers. I preferred it to my real name, but Meri, as in happy, kept looking at me with a sharp suspiciousness in her eyes. I really didn't like it, and I wanted it to go away. I wiggled uncomfortably under the blue and white checkered quilt. What are you supposed to say when the truth is too scary to tell? I didn't know, so I told her only part of the truth and hoped it would be enough.

"My name is Collier," I told her with my arms folded tight across my chest. "But I don't want to be called that. Please don't ever call me that."

Her eyes softened and her mouth eased at the corners. "Well, then, Biker Babe, I think you should get some rest now." She gave my eyebrow one last dab with her towel and stood. She tugged at the quilt, straightening out the wrinkles, and tucked it in tight around my shoulders. "I'll be in the room at end of hallway if you need anything. Just holler." She left me then, closing the door gently behind her.

Meri rolled my bike off the trailer and into the empty stall next to the horse, whose name, she reminded me, was Sergeant. She wouldn't let me help. I was stiff and sore all over, my head hurt, and the Band-Aids pulled, but even so, I felt much better, especially after getting pancakes for breakfast with fresh fruit, orange juice and real brewed coffee. A vast improvement over the sodas and granola bars that I'd been living on for the last three weeks. Gas stations rarely have anything edible in their vending machines.

Sergeant poked his head in through the side window and sniffed at the dangling mirror, his huge nostrils flaring wide. The mirror started swaying, and Sergeant's eyes went big and round. He rolled his ears flat against his head. It looked so funny that I laughed. I shouldn't have. It sent stabbing pains through my head. Meri looked up from where she was trying to get the bent kickstand to lock in to place.

"What's funny?" she asked.

"Nothing really," I said pressing a palm against my temple. "It is strange, though, if you think about it, that there's twelve hundred horses sitting next to just one, and they both fit in the same size stall." Sergeant snorted and tossed his head, obviously not appreciating the comparison. Meri gave the kickstand an extra hard jiggle and it snapped into place. She shoved a board underneath the foot and let the bike lean.

"Twelve hundred?" she asked. "That's a powerful engine." She dusted off her hands. "A light bike with a big engine. I bet it goes fast."

"Very fast," I said. "It'll top two hundred, but if you do that, the wind will blow you right out of the seat. Last week I had it going one-twenty-five on a flat stretch in Kansas. That was scary enough for me."

Meri tucked her hands into the front pockets of her blue jeans and frowned at the bike. "And why, exactly, did you need to go that fast?" The sharp look was back in her eyes, her face almost pinched with it.

I didn't answer but walked around the bike, studying it critically. An air hose was loose and some wires were hanging. I tugged on them a little and then reached over to unlatch the seat. It swung open and I took the tool kit out from underneath. "Soonest started is soonest sung."

"What does that mean?" she asked.

"It means that the sooner I start on these repairs, the sooner I can get out of your hair." My words came out a little harder than I meant them, but I didn't apologize. I chose a star bit screwdriver from the kit and, with a groan for all my aches and pains, sat down cross-legged in the hay. I began loosening the screws from around the engine guard, pointedly ignoring her. I didn't care what she thought of me or the bike or the leather. I'd be leaving, tomorrow at the latest, tonight if I could. It didn't matter to me what kind of judgmental conclusions she came to.

She stood very still for a while and then I heard her leave, feet shuffling softly through the hay until they hit the hard-packed dirt outside the barn door. My fingers fumbled and the screwdriver fell into my lap. I bent my head, scrubbing my hands through my hair. Who was I kidding? It was hard, not answering her questions. I wanted to tell her why I was going that fast. I wanted to tell her about the dark sedan with the California plates that kept appearing every time I got onto an interstate and about the two men with crew cuts and scary blank faces at the small diner in Texas and how I was too scared to stop for food after that. I wanted to tell her about the fear that chased me through

21

four states in two days and how I ended up lost on a backcountry road in the middle of the night in the pouring rain. I wanted to tell her what her pancakes really meant to me. She helped me, and I wanted to tell her everything. She seemed so kind, but hard and strong in all the right places. I felt like it would be safe to tell her my secrets, but it wasn't, and I couldn't.

Sergeant blew a big horsy snort against the back of my head, stretched his neck over the side of his stall and leaned over me to nibble on the dangling mirror.

"Thanks," I said, reaching to pat the underside of his jaw, "that's very helpful."

His teeth snapped and, with a sudden twist of his head, he ripped the mirror loose and dropped it into the hay. I looked down into it. A hollow-eyed, bruised and Band-Aided face stared back up at me. It was almost a stranger's face. Sergeant's nose appeared beside my ear. His lips curled over his big square teeth and he whinnied loud enough to make me jump. He sounded very pleased with himself.

The day was fading into late afternoon when Meri came into the barn with a pitchfork and a wheelbarrow full of hay. Sergeant nickered at her from outside the pasture window as she filled his bin. I stood slowly, my bones creaking, muscles stiff and sore. I stretched, lifting onto my toes, fingers reaching to the ceiling. Meri watched me out of the corner of her eye with a carefully composed face. She seemed to be thinking hard about something, and I hoped she wasn't working herself up to demanding that I leave right away. I was having a bit of a problem with the bike.

"You didn't come in for lunch," she said between forkfuls of hay. "You must be starving."

"No, not really." I was too keyed up to think about eating. I wanted to finish and get out of there before she could ask me more questions that I couldn't answer, before she could cut me all to pieces with her sharp eyes. But it wasn't going to happen. I stared at the bike parts strewn across the barn floor.

She laid the pitchfork across the lip of the wheelbarrow and wheeled it into a corner. "How's it going with the bike?" She hung the fork on a peg on the wall and came into my stall dusting off her hands against the legs of her jeans.

"The clutch pedal is bent." I stooped with a grunt, picked it up off the ground and showed it to her.

She glanced at it and looked questioningly at me. "Is that bad?"

"Yes, it is." I dropped it into the hay. It was worse than bad. It was useless. "For the clutch to work, all the gears have to mesh. With the pedal bent, the gears don't fit together right, and they jam. This isn't something I can fix with shoestring and bubble gum." I poked a toe at it. "Not even with duct tape." The remnants of a silver roll still hung from the foot peg.

Meri laughed and I looked up at her in surprise. I must have had a silly expression on my face because she laughed even harder. I grinned at her and shrugged, feeling suddenly shy of the twinkle in her eye.

She took in a sudden sharp breath and let it out with a puff of her cheeks. She gazed around the stall and then back at the bike. "Would you like some tea?" she asked. "Hot tea, I mean, not iced tea."

"Uhm, sure. Tea would be nice." I answered, still grinning a little. "Do I get crumpets too?"

She smiled and brushed a stray piece of hay off her jacket. "No, you can have scones, but only if you say please and thank you."

It took me a second to realize she was teasing. Her expression was light and open, the smile sitting easily on her lips. It was a very different face from the one she was wearing earlier. I liked this one much better. It made me want to laugh.

I dropped her a mock curtsy. "Yes, please, and thank you. I'd be honored to join you for tea and scones." I gestured at my dusty blue jeans. "Will you be requiring me to change? I'm afraid

I didn't bring any tea dresses."

Her mouth slimmed into a half smile and she nodded almost imperceptibly as if somehow I had said exactly what she expected me to say. Her eyes rose to my hair and then roamed slowly down to my boots. "No, there's no need for you to change. You're fine the way you are." She turned abruptly and walked with bouncy steps toward the house.

Something had changed, not a lot, but there was definitely something different. I watched her go, a little confused, but not unhappy to be that way. Whatever it was, it seemed like a good change. Sergeant poked his head in through the window and nudged me with his nose.

"All right," I said to him over my shoulder. "There's no need to get pushy. I'm going."

In the kitchen, I washed my hands very carefully trying to get all the specks of grease out from under my nails. It would be rude to sit down to tea with dirty fingernails. I couldn't do anything about looking like a Hell's Angels reject, but I didn't want her to think me uncouth. Meri lay out the tea and, true to her word, there were scones, fresh baked and still steaming hot. She poured tea into my mug, and the orangey smell of it made me sigh.

"Pekoe?" I asked wrapping my hands around the warmth. She nodded and passed me the sugar bowl. I spooned, stirred and took a grateful sip. It wasn't until I was halfway through the cup and well into the third scone that I noticed the way she was watching me. Her expression was patient but expectant, like she was waiting for me to do or say something particular. I put the half-eaten scone back down on my plate.

"That clutch part, the one that's bent, isn't going to be easy to get," I said to her.

She smiled and shrugged.

The beginnings of a frown pulled at my Band-Aids. "I'll have to order it. It will probably take about a week to get here."

24

She sipped her tea and stared at me, her funny eyes twinkling a lake-water blue over the rim of her mug. I frowned harder.

"If you don't want me here that long, you can drive me to a motel or something. I can come back when the parts come in."

She put her mug down on the table. "I don't mind you staying here, Bea. As a matter of fact, I think you probably should. You need some time to rest and heal."

I raised an eyebrow, the one that didn't hurt so much.

"Your head." She gestured. "I wouldn't be at all surprised if you had a concussion, and if you won't see a doctor, at least you shouldn't be moving around too much. Besides, the nearest town of any size is over an hour away in the next valley. I don't think they have a good enough hotel there anyway."

"Good enough for what?" I asked. Her cheeks flushed a deep red. She shrugged slightly and touched a finger to the rim of her cup. Her eyes were much too bright. She was pleased about something, almost giddy, like maybe fortune had just dropped a golden egg right into her lap.

Maybe it had. My heart sank through the floor. "You know who I am."

She nodded her head once. "Yes," she said in a soft, contented whisper, a silly shy smile twitching at her lips. She leaned back in her chair. "I'm sorry it took me so long. I'm a little out of touch with the rest of the world. I don't like television very much. I do have one, but it's in the hall closet behind the winter coats. My Aunt Beatrice likes to watch television, though. She watches all the talk shows." Her smile went all crooked and funny. "She says they're all still talking about you." She tipped her mug and looked into her tea. "You did look familiar to me, there in the barn, like I'd seen your picture somewhere before, but I was thinking it was from the wanted posters in the post office. It didn't occur to me that it might be from a supermarket tabloid." She swirled the tea around in her mug. "You can understand that, right? I mean, you did look pretty fierce with all that blood and torn leather ... in a frighteningly beautiful kind of way." Her look was shy and

25

hesitant.

I stared at her. Tea and scones and polite admiration. She was giving me what she thought I wanted, or what she thought I was used to, but she couldn't have been more wrong. I kept staring at her with my teeth clenched together, my face set so tight that the Band-Aids pinched. The smile faded from her face and the silence grew between us. She began tapping her fingers against the side of her mug while I sat there and said nothing.

She sniffed and then cleared her throat. "I made your bed this morning."

"And?"

"And I knocked your bags over," she said looking at the table.

"On purpose?"

Her eyes flickered up, touched mine and then fell back down. "Not exactly on purpose. Not at first, anyway, but they fell and..." She shifted uncomfortably in her chair and then made a sharp, almost angry gesture with her hand. "Okay, fine. I dug through your bags on purpose. I'm sorry. I know it was an invasion, but you have to understand what it's like to live alone. I had to make sure you weren't somebody really bad. Your bags sort of fell over and all that money spilled out with a huge pair of very sharp scissors, and, well, I guess it scared me some, so I kept looking." She wrinkled her nose. "You really need to do some laundry."

I shut my eyes tight and counted to ten to loosen the tightness in my chest. It didn't work. Fear crawled up from my stomach and lodged in my throat. Ever since Kansas, I hadn't been able to stop anywhere long enough to eat a decent meal, much less do laundry. Of course, I hadn't planned on stopping here either, but here I was. I opened my eyes again.

"So, now you know I'm not someone really bad," I said, though I thought that point was debatable, "or at least I'm not someone from a wanted poster. What about you?"

She looked at me surprised. "I'm not on any posters."

I nodded. "Good to know."

"That wasn't what you meant, though, was it?"

26

I lifted a hand to run it through my hair. It was shaking. I put it in my lap. "What I'd like to know is what you intend to do." I watched her watching me until she flushed and looked down into her tea. "I'm sure my family is offering money to anyone who can tell them where I am."

"A lot of money," she agreed without looking up. "More than I've ever seen." Her shoulders twitched in a hint of a shrug. "My family's never had much. It's hard for me to fathom how just the sight of you can be worth a hundred thousand dollars and how it can be worth half a million to get you back." She shook her head at the thought. "And I'm the blindest bat in the valley. I should have recognized you right off. The name Collier sure rang a bell, but I didn't put it all together until I saw your driver's license. I had to call Aunt Beatrice just to make sure I wasn't dreaming. Sure enough, you really are you."

"Did you tell your aunt that I was here?"

"No," Meri said with a slim smile and a shake of her head. "She would've thought I was pulling her leg. Rumor has you hiding out in Chicago." She studied my face. Her eyes wandered all over me until it was my turn to shift uncomfortably in my chair.

"You know, I've seen pictures of you in magazines and stuff," she said, "but they all show you with long hair and dressed in fancy clothes going to fundraisers or banquets or balls. With your face all cut up and . . ." She waved her hand at me sitting there in a borrowed sweatshirt and dusty blue jeans. "I guess it's not so surprising that I didn't recognize you."

Her eyes turned dreamy. "Collier Ann Torrington." She said my name like she was reading it off a marquee. "Half of America is running around trying to spot you, like you were Elvis or something, and here you are right here in Laurelvalley. I've got the missing million-dollar bride sitting right here in my kitchen, drinking tea." She was grinning wider than if she had just won the lottery.

I felt my shoulders sag as all the bone-tired weariness crept back into me. "It's been almost a month. I thought there would

27

be less of an uproar by now."

Meri shook her head. "Your departure was so spectacular and your disappearance so mysterious that the newspeople are milking it for all it's worth. It'll be a month of Sundays before all the excitement dies down."

I leaned back in my chair and looked up at the ceiling, at its patterned tin tiles, and then down at my hands gripped white knuckle tight around my tea mug. "I can't match my father's offer. I didn't bring anywhere near that much money with me, but"—I took in a shaky breath—

"I'll give you all I have if you won't tell him that I'm here for a few days. I'm only asking that you give me long enough to find a way out of here before you call to claim the money."

But I couldn't think of what way that would be, short of stealing a car. There was no way for me to run from here with my bike in pieces, scattered all over her barn floor, and if I had to give her all my money, I wouldn't even be able to catch a bus. Panic started to build at the thought of having to face my father's fury.

It would be terrible.

I looked across the kitchen table at Meri Donovan, gracious host of the formerly missing million-dollar bride, and waited for her answer. She was staring at me with both her eyebrows raised high under her bangs, her mouth open in an 'O' of surprise.

"Good lord, Collier," she said pressing a hand against her chest. "I'm not going to call your family. My Aunt Beatrice would rip me six ways from sundown if I ever did such a thing."

I heard what she was saying, but I kept my hands wrapped tight around the tea mug. It had grown cold, and I couldn't smell the orangey-ness of it anymore.

She leaned across the table and wrapped her hands around mine, trapping them against the side of the mug. "Collier," she said sharply and I jumped. "I'm not going to call your father." She spoke distinctly, her vowels almost smooth except for a funny little twist to her A's.

My head twitched in an abortive shake. It was too hard to

believe. But I wanted to. I wanted to very much. "You're just playing a game. You're trying to keep me here till my father arrives. I bet you've already called him, and he told you to keep me here for as long as you could."

Meri squeezed my hands tighter. "Collier . . . Bea. I haven't called him, and I'm not playing a game. You need help, and I'd like to be the one to help you."

"What about the money?"

"Keep your money, in case something really important comes up. If you start to feel bad about staying here without paying, then you can do chores when your head gets better. This is a farm, remember? I can always use an extra pair of hands."

That wasn't the question I was asking, but her misunderstanding it like that made me feel like maybe she wasn't playing games. Maybe she was telling the truth, but even if she was, then it was only because she didn't understand the consequences.

"What about my father?" I asked. "He won't be happy about you helping me."

She shook her head at me. "He's not going to find you here. You're a big-city girl. Who would think to look for you in a tiny backwoods mountain town?" She gave my hands another squeeze and sat back in her chair. "Stay as long as you need to. You'll be safe here, and I'll be glad for the company."

She was wrong again. For that much money, someone would be sure to find me here, but if she didn't go telling all her friends and neighbors about me, I could be safe for a week, two weeks, or maybe three. That was no small thing. The backs of my hands felt chilled where the warmth of her palms had just been. I opened my mouth to say something, but instead I started to cry. I didn't mean to, but the shame and frustration, the rage and the fear, finally caught up with me. Not just for the last few weeks of running and hiding, but more like for the last twenty-odd years of—never quite successfully—living a life I didn't believe in. Pretending, but never quite enough, to be something I wasn't, all because I had the misfortune of being born into my family, and because, in the end, I failed them so horribly. I wasn't brave enough to be Collier Ann Torrington. I wasn't strong enough to do what was required of me to be my father's daughter.

Meri dragged her chair around the table and set it next to mine. She put her arms around me, fingers lacing through my hair as she held my head to her shoulder and rocked me. "Shhhh," she whispered. "I've got you, hon." Her other hand rubbed gentle circles on my back. "It's all right. You're safe now. I've got you. Shhhh."

Chapter Three: BEGINNINGS

I tinkered with the bike and puttered around the house for the next week or so doing the things that Meri would let me do. It wasn't much. She wouldn't let me help her in the apple orchard, saying that she didn't trust me on a ladder yet, and anyway some of her younger cousins needed something useful to do to keep them out of trouble. About a dozen girls and boys, young men and women, came over almost every afternoon for a week and did all the spring trimming and spraying while I stayed in the house or hid in the barn listening to their loud talk and bright laughter. It seemed so strange to me, their casual joy and quick flares of temper that died an instant after they erupted. My own house was always so quiet, with fear and anger brooding just underneath the patina of polite conversation. Here, Meri's high, clear voice often rose above the others, with the loudest shouts, the loudest laughter, the loudest in song. It was so odd, even a little daunting at first, but I soon found myself wishing that I could be a part of their work, doing something useful, sharing the load, marching to Meri's orders. It would be so easy to fall in with them, if only I could.

Meri did let me take care of Sergeant, brushing him down, turning him out, cleaning and polishing his tack. It was something I knew how to do well, and he seemed to like me fiddling around the barn. He kept blowing on me and nibbling on the bike parts he could reach. He chewed off a rubber handlebar grip. It was on the clutch side. I could live without it.

The days kept slipping slowly by, and the Band-Aids disappeared, one by one, until there were only three left from the original eighteen. I was eating well, heartily even, probably for the first time in my life, and my head was healing fast.

After the day's chores were done, Meri and I spent our evenings together playing cards and board games, laughing too much and talking too loud, trying to paint over the quiet awkwardness that seemed to fall between us as the sun disappeared behind the mountains. She couldn't believe that I had never played Monopoly before, or that I would be so bad at it. I told her that, traditionally, Torringtons weren't very good at playing games that had rules. She gave me a funny look, and we switched over to poker where the rules were a bit more fluid, but I didn't play that very well either. I was good at bluffing, but we played for cashews and I kept forgetting not to eat them.

One evening, the usual April chill turned almost warm and summery. It was so pleasant out that Meri and I decided to sit on the front porch in the wicker swing and make a game out of counting the stars as they came out.

"I see another one," she said, "that makes twenty-six for me."

"How do you know it's not the same one you just counted?"

"I don't," she laughed. "That's part of the game."

"You're cheating!"

"I am not cheating. You wanted a game with no rules, so how can I be cheating when there aren't any rules?"

"That's not fair," I complained.

"It's not about fair," she said, knocking my knee with hers. "That's the whole point of it."

"Why isn't it about fair, do you think?" I asked her seriously. "It seems to me that life should be fair. Everyone should get an equal chance to make what they can out of it."

"That's easy to say when you've got the deck stacked in your favor." Her tone said that she was joking, but I didn't think she was.

"I've heard that one before," I said, looking out toward the darkening line of trees that bordered the road. "But, you know, it's only half true and the half that's true is double-edged and tricky."

"A fool and his money, you mean?"

"Something like that," I said, nodding my head. "Money doesn't change who you are. Having more money only gives you more choices. More choices give you more opportunities to make the wrong choices. The more wrong choices you make, the more twisted your life becomes until you can't tell up from down or right from wrong."

She glanced at me, eyebrows raised at the bitterness in my voice. "Bea, do you have any regrets?"

"About leaving?" I asked and she nodded her head. "No. I didn't belong there."

She kicked out with her feet and started the swing swaying back and forth. "Aunt Beatrice said that the talk shows were all saying how brilliant your marriage was going to be, the merging of old and new money fortunes, a healing of the political divide and all that."

"That sounds like something my father would say."

"It's what the TV people were saying." She looked up at the pale sliver of moon. "He was very good looking, your fiancé."

"He was an asshole of the first water, deeply in love with his polo ponies and, as it's rumored, two underage congressional pages." The bitterness surprised even me this time. I shook my head and looked down at my toes. "I can't believe I just said that."

"What's it like, Bea," she asked abruptly, "to be really, really rich?"

I shivered a little, though the night air was still gentle and warm. "I don't really know. I've never had very much money of my own." I hugged my arms to myself. "What's it like to be really, really happy?"

"I don't know," she answered, her face looking sad in the twilight. "My life has always been a bit of a struggle trying to balance the things I want against the things that other people tell me I should want." She smiled then, a thin, grim little smile. "Aunt Beatrice is always telling me that I shouldn't live here alone, that I should get married and have children so there would always be someone around to help with the farm."

"Why haven't you?"

"Because I think that's a really stupid reason to get married. And anyway, I don't want to." She shrugged. "I guess I haven't found the right person yet."

"What about your parents?" I asked, thinking of all the family pictures that hung on the stair wall. "What do they say you should do?"

Her feet stopped moving and the swing went still. She blinked at the moon. "Both my parents died in a car accident."

"Oh. I'm sorry. I didn't know."

"It was almost five years ago," she said, tossing her head. "I think I've adjusted."

"But you're still not happy to live here in such a beautiful place? Not even with Sergeant, the amazing motorcycle eating horse?"

Meri shook her head slowly. "I wasn't. I love Sergeant and wouldn't give him up for anything, but sometimes it gets so lonely here. I love this place, but farming wasn't what I intended to do with my life." She looked at me with a sideways glance. "I went to college, you know." She looked down again. "Nothing fancy, just a small state college."

I grinned at her. "I went to a big fancy college, all ivy and old bricks, professors with long white beards and big bushy eyebrows. And those were the women."

Meri chuckled and my heart flipped around in a funny way. I hated seeing her look sad, and it made me happy to hear her laugh, even at a bad joke.

"I was an English major," she said. "I love to read, and I sure did get to read a lot. It was fun, in a way. There was so much to learn. But it was scary, too, because I had no idea what kind of job I'd be able to get. I only knew that it wouldn't be farming."

"All I learned was how to pretend to be a snob so I could blend in better. I didn't even major in anything specific, just general studies. There wasn't any point since my whole life had already been planned out for me."

"I had my whole life ahead of me." Meri reached out, touched one of the chains holding the swing, and then tucked her hand in her lap. "This place is all I have left of my parents. I don't have brothers or sisters. If I don't take care of it, nobody will."

She kicked out hard with her foot and the swing wobbled back and forth. I kicked too and set it back into its smooth, swaying rhythm. She grinned with a wide Cheshire smile, leaned into me and patted my knee. She let her hand rest there. I looked down at it. It was solid and warm and I liked it being there, but it scared me, too. This was a very different place from what I knew, and things might not mean what I wished they meant. I sat stiffly, looking out at the twinkling stars, now far too many to count, until her hand twitched. It started to slide slowly off my knee, but I put my hand on top of hers and pressed it against my leg. She smiled again without looking at me. Then, even knowing it would be a mistake, I slipped my arm around her.

Just a week later a crazy north wind blew in from the arctic bringing with it a rare hard freeze. The temperature dropped as the sun went down, and frost began to creep across the window panes. I shivered inside my leather jacket as I jogged back to the house after putting a blanket on Sergeant and kissing him goodnight on the soft pelt of his nose. I spared a sad thought for all the poor wildflowers still bobbing and shivering in the fields as the cold leaked past all my zippers and buttons. I grumbled to myself with teeth chattering, "It's April . . . friggin' April. It's not supposed to be eighty degrees below zero." I was almost sorry that the last of the Band-Aids were gone. I didn't have a hat, and my head would have been warmer with something to cover it.

Inside wasn't much better. The house was exactly what I expected an old house to be in the winter, barely insulated, drafty and cold. I didn't bother to take my jacket off as Meri handed me a mug of hot apple cider.

"How do you stand this all winter?" I asked huddling over the steam.

She shook her head. "It's not like this all winter. It only stays around zero for about a week near the end of January. The rest of the time it's not too bad if you wear long underwear and a couple of layers." She waved her hand in the air. "This will pass. Tomorrow, it will probably be in the sixties." She reached over and rubbed my arm. "When winter really rolls around again, we'll have to get you a better coat."

I watched the steam curl up from the surface of the cider. The cup was warm against my fingers, but my hands still felt chilled to the bone. I wouldn't be seeing winter roll around again, not here anyway, but I couldn't stop myself from wondering what kind of coat she would have picked out for me. Maybe something in a bright checkered plaid with sheep fuzz around the collar. It would have been fun having a coat like that. I watched her standing there in the cold kitchen wearing just one shirt and a light cable-knit sweater looking as comfortable as spring. "How come you're not as cold as I am?"

"I guess your body gets used to it." She laid an almost hot palm against my frosty cheek. "If you're really that cold you should go to bed and get under a pile of quilts. There's a whole bunch of them in the cedar chest in your room."

Without another word, I shoved the cider into her hands and ran for the stairs, her laughter trailing behind me. True enough, the cedar chest was packed with a rainbow of quilts. I threw two of them on the bed, shrugged out of my jacket and boots, sweater and jeans, and burrowed underneath.

Hours later, I was still shivering with frozen fingers and icicle toes. It was too cold to sleep. I got out of bed and put on an extra pair of socks. A soft wind was moaning through the attic rafters. The half moon shone through the branches of an old oak tree standing outside my window, tossing frantic silver shadows on the wall. I grabbed a quilt off the bed, wrapped it around me and paced. There wasn't much room for it. Four steps to the dresser and four steps back, floorboards creaking every first and third. Not enough room really, so I decided to pace in the hallway. I opened my door to see Meri standing in front of hers in her flannel nightshirt, hair tousled and blinking sleepily.

"I heard the floor squeaking," she said. "You can't sleep?"

I shook my head.

"Too cold?"

I nodded.

"Come on in here," she said, opening wider the door to her room.

I followed her in with the train of my quilt rubbing the floor behind me. She stood by her bed and held up the edge of the covers, gesturing for me to get in. I hesitated, and she stood there patiently, her face carefully neutral. I wasn't sure what it meant for me to get into her bed or even if it meant anything at all. This wasn't California. Maybe here people held hands and shared beds all the time just for comfort's sake. Maybe friends patted each other on the knees and cuddled on the porch swing every fine summer evening and that was all it was.

The thought made me feel squirmy inside. I was very good at pretending to think or not to think, to feel or not to feel, but I didn't want to have to do that here. Not in this place. I shivered with the cold of the floorboards soaking through my socks. Mery raised an eyebrow at me. She was right. It was too cold to worry about any of that now. I threw my quilt on top of her bed and crawled under the covers. She slipped in behind me and snuggled against my back, throwing a loose arm around my middle. I was under three quilts now, and her body was hot where it pressed against me. It felt good to be there, wrapped snug against the cold, with her solid weight resting behind me.

It felt too good. I started to grow warm in uncomfortable places, and I shivered again. Meri pressed in tighter against me, folding her arm across my chest, tucking her thighs against the backs of mine. So much of her skin was touching me. I'd never slept with someone like this before. I shouldn't be doing it now, but I would never get to sleep if I went back to my room. I smiled at myself. That was very nearly a lie, but it was close enough to true to live with. Whatever this did or didn't mean to her, it seemed wrong to reject the comfort she was offering or to deny how bad I wanted it. I hugged her arm against my chest and relaxed into her. She sighed deeply, and I felt her relaxing, too.

I was almost asleep when she rolled away from me, but before I could get cold again, she reached behind her and tugged at my arm. I rolled over and slipped a hesitant hand around her waist. She pulled my arm tighter, pressing me hard against her back. My nose ended up buried in a thick tangle of her hair. It smelled of cinnamon and warm apple cider. That woke me up. She pulled my arm tighter and tucked my hand underneath her chin wrapping her fingers around mine. I could feel her ribs moving underneath my arm, the slight shifting of a flannelled breast against my wrist, the rhythmic pressing of her back against my chest. A slow ache began to build inside me.

I was far more than warm now, and I was wide-awake. I lay there staring into her hair, the blond of it almost glowing in the moonlight, counting her breaths, timing mine to hers, my stomach pushing against her back, hers pushing against my elbow. I counted until I reached one thousand and her breathing had deepened into a steady rhythm. Slowly, I lifted my head and rubbed my lips against the soft flannel of her shoulder. The material shifted and I let my lips press against the warmth of her bare skin. She stirred softly inside her dream and pressed my hand over her heart.

The morning found me freezing and alone. I shivered underneath the quilts for a while, unwilling to get out of bed, but both nature and duty called. I got up, took a fast shower and dressed. I made her bed as best I knew how and went downstairs to the kitchen where I could smell bacon frying. Meri was standing over the stove.

She turned and smiled when she heard me come in. "Here," she said, handing me the spatula, "if you finish the bacon, I'll take care of Sergeant."

I smiled at her gratefully, glad for the opportunity to miss the frosty morning, and grabbed the spatula. She didn't let go. She slid her hand slowly up the handle and over mine, leaned into me and kissed me lightly on the lips. I stared at her in stunned silence, my mouth hanging open. With a grin, she chucked me under the chin and my teeth snapped shut. She grabbed her coat off the back of the chair and sauntered out the door, on her way to the barn. I stared at the door and then turned to the bacon, scowling at the bubbling strips as I shifted them around in the pan. Her kiss burned my mouth and made me feel all shaky inside, but Meri was the last person in the world that I wanted to hurt. She didn't understand, and I didn't know how to explain.

When she came inside, her face flushed with the cold, I had the slightly burned bacon on the table along with some mostly overdone eggs. The toast sat chilled and forgotten in the toaster. I poured her a cup of coffee and sat in my chair opposite hers, keeping my head lowered, unwilling to meet her eyes but still feeling the weight of them on me. I sat with my hands in my lap, listening to the scratching of her fork against her plate, the creak of her chair as she shifted her weight, the faint scuff of her shoes against the floor. I had never been so aware of her or been so frightened of myself.

"Bea," she said. I looked up, reluctantly. Her eggs were scattered but uneaten. She sat slumped in her chair. "I'm sorry," she said. "I guess I was out of line. I must have misinterpreted . . ." She stopped and cleared her throat. "When you kissed my shoulder last night, I thought . . . I must not have understood . . ." Her voice broke, and she dropped her fork. "I'm sorry," she said again, pushing her chair back, legs screeching loudly against the tile. Her feet pounded up the stairs. I heard her door slam shut.

I sat, staring at her plate, then rose, gathered the dishes and took them to the sink. The house was creaking and popping as the air outside began to warm, but underneath it, I thought I heard her crying. It was too late, then. I hurt her already.

I carefully washed the dishes and put them in the rack to dry. Egg chunks swirled around in the sink and disappeared down the drain. I left the toast sitting popped up in the toaster. Moving slowly, I dried my hands, put the plate of bacon in the refrigerator and turned the coffeepot off. It was time for me to leave. Past time. I had to go now, before things got really out of hand, before I hurt her any more, before I hurt myself. The only thing left was to figure out how. I hadn't the faintest idea how to go about stealing a car, or maybe Meri would be willing to drive me to a bus station. I slumped against the counter and rubbed at my eyes. There was still one other thing that I had to do before all that, harder than asking for a ride, harder than stealing a car. I had to find a way to tell her good-bye.

I climbed the stairs with heavy feet, past the pictures of her family that hung on the wall every three steps or so, then walked to the end of the long hall. I knocked on her door. "Meri?" I called through the pine.

"Yes?" I heard her sniff and blow her nose.

I closed my eyes and leaned against the door. "Can I come in?"

40

"Yes."

I opened the door. She was lying on the bed curled on her side with a tissue balled in her hand. Three more lay crumpled on the nightstand. I went in and sat on the edge of the bed next to her knees. She looked so small curled up like that, looking at me with tear-brightened eyes. I reached over to tuck a stray wisp of hair back behind her ear. I let my hand linger, tracing the outline of her ear, the line of her jaw, touching her cheek with my fingertips, wiping the dampness from the bridge of her nose.

"I'm sorry," she said again and left it there.

I shook my head. "There's nothing for you to be sorry about, Meri. This is my fault. The mistake was mine. I knew you didn't understand, and I didn't make any effort to explain."

"Are you going to leave now?" Her voice broke.

I pulled a new tissue from the box and handed it to her. "I have to, Meri. I should have left weeks ago."

"You should have left before I screwed everything up."

"You didn't screw anything up."

"I know I did, Bea. You don't have to soften it." She balled the new tissue in her hand and dabbed at the corner of her eye. "I've gotten so used to you. I guess I started making assumptions that I shouldn't have. I forgot you're not from around here. People do things differently where you come from. You're probably used to all that causal touching and stuff, and then I had to go and think it meant something different, something more."

I looked down at her, so surprised that I wasn't sure whether to laugh or to cry. I didn't do either. I touched a finger to the corner of her mouth and ran it lightly across her lips. It made all my fingertips tingle.

"It did mean something more, Meri." Her eyes widened a little as I cupped her cheek in my hand. "I love being here with you. If I could, I would stay here forever."

She laid her hand over mine and pressed my palm hard against her face. "You can, Bea. I want you to."

I shook my head. "No, I can't."

"Why?" She turned her head and whispered into my palm. "If it meant something more, why can't you stay?"

"Because my life is complicated and yours is not." I rubbed my thumb gently across her cheekbone. "Because you're good and kind and strong, and I'm none of those things. I've already failed so many people, Meri. I can't stand the thought of failing you. I can't stay because I can't be what you need me to be."

Meri dropped my hand and sat up, her face only inches away from mine. "That's just plain silly, Bea. I don't want you to be anything that you're not being right this minute." Her eyes, storm cloud gray and glimmering, searched across my face. She lifted a hand and touched my forehead, running her fingers lightly along my scar. "I want you to stay here with me. That's all. You've become a part of this place. You belong here now."

I shook my head and her hand fell away. "You don't understand, Meri. If I stay, someone will find me."

"Bea, you're in the middle of nowhere. No one's going to find you."

"Ever?" I asked. "Do you plan on keeping me locked in the pantry when you have guests?" She didn't answer and I nodded slightly. "Someone will find me, and if they find me here then it won't just be me that pays the price." I touched her cheek with the back of my hand. "I don't think I could stand that. It's too beautiful here for you to let me mess it up."

"I want you to mess it up," she whispered fiercely.

"Only because you don't understand what that can mean."

She leaned forward, dipped her head and rubbed her lips across my shoulder. She turned her head so that her mouth lay warm and damp against my throat. "I know what *that* means." The words whispered across my skin in a tickle of breath that raised goose bumps on my arms.

I closed my eyes and shivered. She raised her head and rubbed her cheek against mine. The soft warmth of her nearly choked me. Her fingers were on my chin, turning my head. She laid her mouth on mine, a gentle brush of lips, palms sliding up to cup my cheeks. I took in the smell of her, barnyard and springtime, frost and fresh air. A hint of cinnamon still hung in her hair. She made a small sound and her mouth opened slightly. I opened mine, and the taste of her drew an echo from me. She pressed harder and I leaned into her kiss. The tip of her tongue touched mine and our mouths melted together.

Her hands dropped and fumbled at my waist, pulling at my sweater, slipping underneath my shirts. Her palms were cool against my skin. One hand pressed hard against the small of my back and the other slid over my ribs. It moved higher, sliding slowly like scuffed silk over my skin, until she held my breast in the cup of her hand. She squeezed, and I groaned into her mouth. She groaned into mine. I wrapped my arms around her and pressed her tight against me. I was lost. It was too late to stop this thing, even though I knew it was a mistake. It was the wrong path to take. It would only hurt her in the end, and that would hurt me, but I couldn't stop my feet from stepping.

"We shouldn't do this, Meri," I said, kissing a long slow line down the side of her neck, my hands clutching at her back.

"Yes, we should," she said and pulled us down.

I woke with a smile and a lazy cat stretch, my body languid and pleasantly sore in some very odd places. The late afternoon sun beamed in through the window, and I rolled over to touch Meri, to feel the warm brush of her skin, to make sure the whole morning hadn't been a dream. She wasn't there, only cold sheets and a rumpled pillow. I sat up.

"Meri?" I called out, looking frantically around the room for my clothes. Or any clothes. They weren't on the floor where we left them this morning. There was no bra caught on the bedpost, no panties hanging from lampshade. "Meri?" I called out again.

"Coming," I heard her call from downstairs. "Don't get up. I'm coming right back."

I lay down again against the pillows, shivering at the chill, and snuggled the comforters around my shoulders. I heard Meri clomping up the stairs. She appeared in the doorway holding a tray with two steaming mugs and a plate of toast.

I smiled at her shyly. "You didn't have to do that."

"Yes, I did," she said setting the tray on the nightstand and handing me a cup of coffee. She sat on the edge of the bed, leaned over and kissed me lightly. "I didn't want to be the only one with coffee breath."

She did have coffee breath, and her clothes smelled of fresh air and barn waste. I inhaled deeply, filling myself with her scents, holding the essence of her deep inside me. If only I could keep her there, but a body has to breathe. I let the breath trickle out slowly. She smiled at me and shook her head as if she knew what I was doing. Maybe she did. Her sharp eyes didn't miss much. I took a sip of my coffee and pulled her to me, kissing her hard, urgent and insistent. She took the cup out of my hands, set it on the tray and slipped under the covers. She pulled me against her, sweater scratching at my breasts, jeans chafing at my thighs. Her boots knocked against my shin.

I grinned at her. "I hope you're not getting barn muck all over your sheets."

"Who cares?" she asked as her lips nibbled a shivery trail across my shoulder.

I slipped a hand underneath her sweater. She hadn't bothered with a bra. My thumb brushed lightly over a taut nipple. I pressed it gently and she moaned against my skin. I felt my body swell and tighten.

"I only mention it," I said softly, my mouth against her ear, "because I'm not sure how I'm going to get your jeans off if you still have your boots on."

Her shoulders shuddered under my hands. She raised her head to look at me. "You're naked." She slid her hand slowly down the length of my body, cupping my butt and pulling me tighter against her. "That's good enough." She moved her hips forward and back, up and then down. The rough cloth of her jeans rubbed across the center of me making the breath catch in my throat. She bent her head to kiss me, but I pulled away. "What?" she asked.

I tugged at her sweater. "Off."

She smiled and slipped the sweater over her head. I bent to kiss her breasts. She gasped as I touched her with my tongue, rolled the tight bud of her around in my mouth. Her hand slid through my hair, cradling the back of my head, holding me to her. I sucked harder, taking as much of her breast into my mouth as I could. She cried out, a mangle of half-formed words, then she lifted my head and pulled me up to press her mouth hard against mine. Her tongue pushed between my lips as her hand dipped between my legs, fingers sliding, soft and sure, with a stroke so sweet that I nearly forgot who I was. Her tongue played over mine and my hips moved against her hand, matching her stroke for stroke. The warmth began to build inside me, a quivering, flickering flame in my belly, growing hotter and brighter.

Meri shifted, and a boot smashed against my ankle.

"Ow," I yelled and rolled away from her.

"Oh, Bea, I'm sorry." Meri reached down and rubbed my knee.

"That's not where it hurts," I said, "and you really need to take those boots off."

She kicked them off and I raised an eyebrow at her. "I never did lace them," she said with a wry smile.

"You mean my ankle's all bruised now for no very good reason?"

She grinned at me. "You want me to kiss it and make it all better?"

I started to grin too, but the look in her eyes took the smile right off my face. "Oh, yes."

She lifted herself, straddled my body and, with a quick, hard kiss, ducked underneath the covers. Suddenly, I found it hard to catch my breath with my heart beating so hard against my chest. She slid her body slowly down mine, letting her breasts trail over

45

my skin, across my stomach, over my hips, brushing them down the line of my thighs, pressing against my knees, rubbing across my shins, making my hands spasm and clench. She slid past my feet. Her fingers made little circles around my ankle. "Is this where it hurts?"

I shook my head, forgetting for a moment that she couldn't see me. "It's the other one," I said hoarsely.

Her fingers circled around my other ankle. There was the light touch of her lips on my shin, hands squeezed my foot and began playing lightly over my calves. Then she took my big toe into her mouth. Tongue to toe. I never imagined that I could feel such a thing as the fire that shot up my leg.

"Oh, god!" My body jerked and trembled.

Her hands and mouth moved higher, fingers caressing the backs of my knees, lips trailing close behind. She wriggled between my legs, pushed against my thighs, lifted them and stretched them wide. Her hands slipped under me, scooting under to grab my butt. She lifted me up and into her mouth, drank me down, swallowed me whole. Small noises burst from deep in my throat as my hips moved to match the warm, broad strokes of her tongue. She slipped fingers inside me, and my hands clawed at the sheets. She focused her attentions and narrowed in on the brightest ember in the flames. My body pulsed, shuddered and writhed as the whole world shrank down to rest on the tip of her tongue.

I lay draped between Meri's legs with my cheek pressed against her stomach, her wet still on my chin. The sound of her sharp cries still tingled down my spine. Her fingers played through my hair as I listened to the strong beat of her heart, my toes tapping out its rhythm against the foot of the bed.

"So you'll stay here then, Bea?" she asked softly.

I raised my head to rest my chin in the dip of her bellybutton. Evening was falling, and the room was growing dim, but her hair

46

still glowed brightly as it lay in a scattered mess across the pillow. "Yes, I'll stay," I answered, "for as long as I can."

She lifted her head. "I don't understand."

I kissed the soft skin of her stomach and moved from between her legs to stretch out next to her. "I'll stay until my father finds me. He will, you know. He always has."

"So?" She shrugged. "He finds you and you tell him that you're staying here with me. What can he do?"

"That's the question, isn't it?" I touched her skin, my fingers drawing little spirals over her heart, over the swell of her breast and then in between. "I've seen him do nasty things to get what he wants, hurtful, underhanded but perfectly legal things." I'd also seen him do things that were on the wrong side of legal, but I didn't see any point in sharing. I was afraid enough for her already.

"But what can he do to you? You don't need his money." She turned her head away from me, her eyes blinking. "I mean, I'm not rich or anything but I'm sure not going to let you starve. You don't need him if you don't mind living on a farm."

I touched her chin and turned her face back toward me. "My father wouldn't hesitate to hurt the things I love to get me to do what he wants me to do." Meri didn't say anything, just blinked at me. I grinned at her. "That would be you."

And a smile lit up her face that brightened my whole world. Her eyes sparkled as she grabbed my hand and kissed my fingers. "I love you too, Bea."

"I know," I said squeezing her hand. "That's why when he comes, I'll have to leave, so he won't hurt you."

Her smile faded. "You've already run clear across the country. Where else is there for you to go?" She pressed my hand against her chest. Her heart beat hard in the center of my palm. "Bea, stay here. Stand up to him. Face him down. We'll do something to make him leave us alone."

My fingers found the dip in her skin right at the hollow of her throat. It was so soft. "Do you know what would happen if the zoning laws for your farm were suddenly changed?" Meri looked confused at my sharp left turn, so I answered the question for her. "You would be forced to sell your land."

Understanding widened her eyes and then disbelief narrowed them again. "No one can force you to sell something you don't want to."

"Yes, they can," I said, drumming my fingers on her collarbone. "It's perfectly legal for the government to force you to sell your property to them as long as they pay you a fair market value and promise to use the property for the greater good. What do you think would happen if my father waltzed in here with a few million and pledged to build a hospital or a library or a new school, but insisted that it be built on this piece of land?"

She thought about that for a minute and then shook her head. "Harvey would never do that to me. He would never let it happen."

"Who's Harvey?"

"He's what we have here in Laurelvalley that passes for a mayor. He pretty much runs this town even though we're not much of a town. He's a good man, and he's known me since I was born. He knows what this place means to me, and he would never try to take it away."

"You have a lot of faith in him."

"Yes, I do, but it's not just that. This is a very small place. I mean, Laurelvalley covers a lot of acreage, but there aren't that many people. If you stub your toe and cry out loud, everyone knows about it before the sun sets. If Harvey tried to do an underhanded deal, he'd be run out of town before the ink was dry."

I shrugged. "Then my father would get the state to do it, and this town would get punished as well. How would everyone feel about a municipal trash dump being located here, a high security state prison or a toxic waste burial site to foul your streams and rivers?"

She lifted her head from the pillow. "He could really do

that?"

"He's done it before. How do you think Yucca Mountain happened? Someone made him angry and now they have a nuclear waste dump in their backyard."

"And he could do that here?"

"If he thought the matter was important enough, he could pull enough strings to make something bad happen."

"And it's so very important to him that you marry some guy you barely know and like even less?"

I rolled onto my back and stared at the ceiling. It sounded so stupid when she put it that way. "It's not just that."

"What is it then?"

I turned my head to look at her. "There were deals riding on me, long-term deals, things my father had been building toward for years. There were schemes and plans, plans within plans. It wasn't just a marriage. It was a truce between two warring families, an alliance between rival factions. The marriage was their reason to come together. Without it, any deals they make with each other will make them look like traitors to their friends and weak to their enemies."

But it was more than that. It had been the beginnings of a plan to wrest power away from the conservative extremists and put the reigns of the government back into the hands of the conservative centrists by bringing two of the largest rival factions together through a common ground. I would have been that common ground and the bridge over the last chasm that blocked my father's presidential ambitions. It was the whole reason I'd been born. But I didn't know how to explain that to Meri, who kept her television in the hall closet and rarely considered the world out past the farm gate. Meri's expression was quizzical, and I knew she didn't really understand.

"I hurt him, Meri. I queered his deal. I embarrassed him socially. He lost money, he lost opportunities, and he lost his only child."

Meri rolled onto her side and rested her head in the palm of her hand. "Does he really care so much about that only child?" she asked with something dangerously close to pity in her eyes. It made things move all wrong inside my chest.

"I wish I knew," I answered softly. "I've never been very clear on what he does and doesn't care about. I do know that he cares about what the future will say about him. He cares about his legacy and the continuation of his legitimate line to watch over it. No grandchildren, no line." I reached for her hand and raised it to my mouth. "If he knew about this," I said brushing her knuckles lightly across my lips, "I don't know what he'd do, but it would be something awful."

She stretched out a finger and touched my cheek. "You've been hiding what you are all your life, haven't you?"

"I don't know what I am. I've never dared to put a label on it for fear that the ground might open and swallow me whole. That's what my father says should happen to people with un-natural affections." I squeezed her hand. "It doesn't feel so un-natural, though."

"Am I the first woman you've ever been with?" she asked, smiling shyly. "Slept with, I mean."

"You're the first woman I've ever dared to kiss." I turned my head to kiss the finger softly stroking my cheek. "But you're not the first woman I've wanted to kiss."

She blew out a slow breath between pursed lips. "That must have been horrible for you, to live like that."

I nodded. "It was hard, but it was also absolutely necessary. My father's power base is very conservative. He says what he thinks they want him to say, so he speaks loud and often against gay people. He says it's a mental illness and we should all be institutionalized. I don't know what he really believes, but if the media got wind that his only daughter was gay, it would be a circus. He gets very angry with anyone who gives his enemies a stick to hit him with."

Meri twined her fingers around mine. "I think I'm beginning to see the true size of our problem."

50

She had no idea. "It's not our problem, Meri. It's just mine."

"No. You're wrong about that." Meri grabbed my chin and pulled my face to hers. "It is our problem. You belong here. I have no intentions of letting you go, and that's the end of it." She laid a finger against my lips.

I shifted my head and bit gently on the tip of her finger. "You 'ave to," I said through my teeth, "dere are bigger t'ings at stake dan jus us." I closed my lips around her finger, circled it with my tongue and slid it slowly out of my mouth.

She let go of my chin. "Are you talking about the farm?" A note of worry crept into her voice.

"I'm talking about this whole town. He could turn everything around us inside out. It wouldn't be right for me to stay here for my own comfort's sake and let everyone around me suffer for it."

She looked at her damp finger and then closed her fist around it. "So, you're just going to keep running?" Her eyes glittered in the dim light.

"Yes." I wrapped my hands around her fist and uncurled her fingers. "There are no other real options. Everything else is just wishing." I laid a kiss on her open palm.

"But where can you go from here?"

I looked back up at the ceiling. It was very familiar to me now. The old plaster was lumpy in places. It caught the orange rays of the setting sun and threw odd oblique shadows across it. "I was thinking about driving to Florida and catching the next space shuttle to Mars."

Meri laughed softly, sadly. "There's no way we could scrape up enough money for that, and besides, once you got to Mars, you'd just have to turn around and come home again."

"Oh, damn. I hadn't thought about that."

She put her hand on my stomach, fingers gently stroking, making things lower clench and grow warm. "Seriously, Bea, when will you stop running? When the bike breaks for good? When you run out of money? When your father dies? When you do?"

My throat tightened. "I don't know, Meri. I don't have any big plans. I can't even see around the next bend. There's no way to know where the road ends."

Meri studied my face with a sad little frown of her own. She lifted my arm, tucked it around her shoulders and snuggled herself against me, her nose nestled against my neck, her knee thrown across my lap. "So what are you going to do?"

I kissed her hair. It still smelled like cinnamon. "I'll finish repairing the bike and then, when he comes, I'll leave."

"And you're so sure he'll come?"

There was a spark of defiance in that question. I wished I had some reassuring words for her, but even though I'd never run so far as this, I'd hidden from him before, and he'd never failed to track me down, whether it was to the linen closet in the nanny's quarters or to a friend's garage two states away.

"Yes, I'm absolutely sure, Meri," I said quietly, and her body sagged against me.

"Will you come back?" she asked, her words a warm tickle against my collarbone.

"Will you want me to?"

"Yes," she said. "This place won't seem right without you."

"Then I'll go, circle around a few times and come back as soon as I can." I squeezed her closer to me, fighting hard to convince myself that it wasn't a lie. Maybe it wasn't, I thought, but it probably was.

"But you'll stay here for now, right?" She tilted her face to me and I kissed her.

"I'll stay right until the last minute." I kissed her again, slower this time and much more thoroughly.

She pulled herself up and slid on top of me. Her legs wriggled between mine, pushing them apart and she pressed herself hard against me. She was still wet and slick.

"Then we should make every minute count." She whispered against my lips. Meri grabbed my shoulders and thrust her hips

52

forward, moved them around in long, slow circle, sliding herself over me.

"Oh, god," was my answer.

Chapter Four: SECRETS

Almost two weeks later, the clutch parts finally came in the mail. It had taken much longer than I expected it to. I didn't dare try using any of my credit cards to order them, so I had to go through some complicated postal order routine. It made me wonder what people used to do in the days before credit cards were invented. While I was waiting for the damn things to arrive, it occurred to me that maybe the simpler life was also sometimes the harder one, and that maybe there were hard parts to every kind of life.

I made some progress in fixing the bike. I could, at least, duct tape the broken plastic parts and reattach loose hoses and wires, but I soon reached a point that was beyond my expertise. I needed tools that weren't included in the standard under-the-seat tool kit, like wrenches and pliers and things. Meri wasn't very helpful. She could drive a tractor, plow a field, bale hay and rewire a light socket, but she didn't know what a socket wrench looked like. She showed me to a shed where her father had kept all his tools. It was on the far side of the pasture away from the barn, near where the old sheep pen was. We walked quickly down the overgrown path, once neatly bricked, now choked and weedy. She pointed to the shed with thin, pressed lips and tight, pinched eyes, turned and walked quickly back to the house.

I watched her go, jealous for just an instance of her grief, and then it struck me, like a hammer to the heart, that I didn't love my father. I was afraid of him. He had bred in me a blind obedience, but that wasn't love. I'd grown up thinking that it was, but I was wrong. Just then, I wished I knew what it felt like to have a protector and not a persecutor, a confessor instead of a judge.

I gave my head a quick shake, shoving away my impossible dreams, and turned to the shed. It was much grayer than the barn. Its moss-shingled roof was cracked and sagging in the middle. The door was swollen in its frame and only opened after a good hard shove of my shoulder. Dust and dirt sifted down from the ceiling. My shoes stirred more from the floor and made me sneeze. I rubbed my nose on my sleeve and looked around at all the neatly hanging tool-shaped lumps of rust. There was a row of different kinds of hammers, saws arranged by size, dozens of screwdrivers, coffee cans nailed to the wall filled with dusty clumps of screws or old empty mouse nests. A battered toolbox sat on the workbench, its lid still open and waiting. There were wrenches inside, all frozen with their jaws clamped tightly shut. A half-made birdhouse sat next to the toolbox, its mouse-gnawed wood dry and cracking. I touched a saw hanging in its place on a wooden peg. Dust and rust came off on my fingers. None of these tools would ever fix anything again. I closed the door behind me as best I could, went back to the house and wrapped Meri in a tight bear hug.

Meri phoned her blue-haired Aunt Beatrice to ask if she knew anybody motorcycle savvy who would be willing to make a house call. Her auntie spent a good ten minutes chewing her out for not calling in over a week. I listened to Meri "yes, ma'am" and "no, ma'am" into the phone, blushing and shifting from foot to foot. I kept snickering at her and she kept shushing me with an abrupt wave of her hand. I had to leave the room to keep from laughing out loud.

In the end, her aunt said she would send over one of the cousins. Meri couldn't tell me any more than that. She couldn't even say if it would be a real blood cousin of some indeterminate remove or just somebody she called cousin for politeness sake. Everyone in Laurelvalley, who wasn't an actual sister or brother, mother or father, was called cousin, aunt or uncle. Meri said that you couldn't tell who was related to whom just by listening to people talk.

She kissed me, shrugged into her jacket and kissed me again as she walked out the door. Aunt Beatrice had bullied her into paying a visit, and since we had lately been reduced to eating pickled mystery stuff from the pantry whose labels had fallen off, she was also going to get some groceries while she was in town and some feed for Sergeant, too.

It was the first time I had been alone in her house for any significant length of time, and, to be honest, it felt strange, almost like I was in the wrong place. It was too quiet without her there. I didn't care for it much, so I went out to the barn where I knew Sergeant would be glad to see me. There was always stuff that needed doing out in the barn.

Sergeant was glad to see me, or it might have been the apple I had in my pocket. I spent most of the afternoon with him, piddling with the bike, changing his straw, braiding red ribbons into his mane, washing slimy horse drool out of the water trough. The sun was low in the sky when I finished with the afternoon chores, and I was just about to shut the barn doors for the evening when a truly ancient pickup truck rolled down the driveway, the kind with the round roofed cab and bug-eyed headlights. Its red paint was so faded that I almost mistook it for a huge hunk of rust on wheels. It was much older even than Meri's decrepit truck, but the engine hummed prettily as it swung off the drive and pulled next to the barn. The man inside waved a hand at me and flashed an easy smile. I didn't wave back since I didn't know who he was or what he wanted. I just watched him. The truck door opened with a tortured screech of metal scraping on metal, and he got out. He was very tall, very broad and almost obscenely muscular. He might have seemed intimidating if it weren't for the lazy slump of his shoulders. He was fairly young, and his face was almost handsome in a rugged fair-haired farm boy kind of way. It was deeply tanned and had just the beginnings of a cragginess that would probably take it over later in his life.

He tipped his ball cap up on his head and held out his hand to me.

"Hey, there. I'm Taylor. I'm looking for the guest with the ailing motorcycle."

I shook his hand. It swallowed mine, but he didn't squeeze very hard. A true Southern gentleman. "The bike's mine. My name's Bea."

"Oh, yeah?" he said flashing his smile again. "Like in Auntie Bea?"

"No, like in the letter B brought to you today by the number ten."

He blinked a few times and then shrugged. Maybe they didn't get PBS in this valley. "Alrighty then," he said. "So, where's the bike?"

I nodded my head at the barn. "It's in there, in the stall next to Sergeant."

He grinned a lopsided smile that made the corners of his eyes burst out into crow's feet. "I'll bet he's enjoying that."

"Seems to be. He keeps eating parts off of it."

Taylor shook his head. "Crazy dumb horse. Well, let's go see what we've got."

We went into the barn and stood in front of the bike. He gave a low whistle and looked at me sideways. "That sure is a lot of bike for such a little slip of a girl."

I raised an eyebrow at him. "I'm pretty tall for a girl."

He shook his head again. "Tall helps your toes touch the ground, but it takes muscle to wrangle a bike like this. You look like you could turn sideways into the wind and disappear."

"You can't wrangle a bike like this," I said with a little bit of sternness. "It'll kill you if you try. It takes finesse to control it, not muscle."

He grunted softly and ran a hand across the scratches on the tank. "Looks like you ran out of finesse on a left turn somewhere."

"I ran into a deer," I said flatly.

He looked at me closer. He eyes went to the scar on my forehead, still pink and puckered, and they widened just a little. He whistled again. "That had to hurt."

"Yes, it did."

He grinned. "You must be tough as a nickel steak."

It was my turn to look puzzled. "I bet you're related to Meri."

His grin dimmed and he pulled the brim of his cap lower over his eyes. "Now, why do you say that?"

"I don't understand half the things she says either."

He nodded his head and then shook it from side to side. "Naw, we're not related. We just grew up together. We've been running around since we were both knee high to a grasshopper. You live in a small town, you pick up funny sayings." He rubbed at his jaw. "I didn't see the truck outside. She's not here?"

"No, she went into town."

He nodded his head, managing to look both relieved and disappointed at the same time. He turned to the bike. "Well, let's see what we're going to need to do to this."

I showed him what I had done and what still needed doing. I handed him the box with the new clutch parts.

"I couldn't put this in myself because I don't have the right tools."

"Yeah," he said absently, opening the box and rummaging around inside it, "it's going to need a torque wrench, at least. I'll have to look up the bike specs."

"There are no bike specs," I said and he gave me a pained look. I shrugged. "It's custom."

"All the way custom?" he asked, eyebrows rising. "From tire to tire?"

I nodded. He lifted his cap and scratched his head. He took a closer look at me and then at the bike. He looked at me again with a new expression in his eyes.

"Wow," he said and settled the cap back on his head. "Who'd have thought?"

My bike was almost like any other sport cruiser with shiny black trim and gleaming chrome. It was sleek and mean. It had sharp lines, but it didn't stand out in a crowd unless you took a close look. At the time, I thought I was being modest. Later, it helped me to run fast without being noticed. I had it special built with an ultra light aluminum frame, a V-4 and all the bells and whistles I could think of that could be tucked away somewhere. I originally intended it as a mild rebellion against my father, spending a truckload of my allowance money on something he wouldn't approve of, but somewhere along the line, I fell in love with the bike. I think that was when my world began to change.

"These might help," I said, handing him the papers that came with the clutch.

"Oh yeah, right," he said setting the box down next to the bike. He took the papers from me and read them over. "That makes things a little easier. I won't have to guess so much." He sat in the hay cross-legged. "Hey, could you go out to the truck and get the tool box that's . . ." He stopped himself and then he frowned. "Never mind," he said getting up.

"What?"

He shrugged and winked at me. "I got to thinking of you being so tough and all that I forgot you were still a girl."

He went out of the stall and I stared after him, feeling slightly indignant. No one had ever said anything like that to me before. I ran my hand through my hair, still short and spiky, but Meri had trimmed it neatly. I looked down at myself. Jeans, boots and a checkered shirt. Okay, not specifically designed to be attractive, but it wasn't awful. It was, in fact, nearly the same thing he was wearing. Oh, I thought, and for the first time since I arrived, I felt vaguely uncomfortable with my clothes. I frowned at the door. Meri never made me feel like that.

He came back in with a huge battered toolbox and set it next to the bike with a clunk. He opened it with a well-practiced snap and dug out a small flashlight, flipped it on and started peering around the engine.

"You got a pretty good start, I see."

"Yes. I did all the easy stuff."

"Not bad. The clamps for the air hose are on backward, but that's not a big deal. Looks like all I need to do is to replace the clutch. You laid it down pretty hard, yeah?" He looked up at me, his eyes moving to the scar on my forehead. "It wouldn't hurt to check it out real good, you know, belt tension, valve adjustments, change all the fluids and stuff. Shouldn't take too long."

"How long do you think?"

"Oh, I don't know, I could probably do it this weekend unless you're in a hurry. I could come over after work tomorrow, but"— he glanced at the single bare overhead bulb—"we'd have to rig some better lights in here."

I was in a hurry and I wasn't. Deep inside I knew that I had already been in one place for far too long. If I were a smart person, I would have him fix the bike now and leave as soon as it was ready, in spite of what I told Meri. But I didn't want to leave, and a broken bike was as good a reason as any not to. Sergeant stuck his head in through the pasture window and nickered. I went over to him and rubbed the white blaze that swirled around between his eyes. I wanted to stay with Sergeant, too. I would miss him. Sergeant stretched out his neck, nickered softly and nipped at a taillight. Taylor reached over and thunked him on the nose. Sergeant snorted hard and his head disappeared.

"Crazy dumb horse," Taylor said wiping horse snot off his cheek.

• • •

The weekend came, and I forgot all about Taylor and the bike. Meri had a way of capturing my attention, which she did right after breakfast. We were doing the dishes together, got a little crazy with the suds and finished the chore wearing most of the lemony fresh dish soap. We took what was left of it and headed upstairs to the shower, and that's where things really got out of hand. I was squeaky clean and still smelled like lemons when I finally made it out to the barn to check on Sergeant late that afternoon. I saw Taylor's truck outside, but, of course, I hadn't heard him come up the drive. He was there in the bike stall, sitting cross-legged in the hay, trying to get the old clutch assembly out of the engine.

Taylor only glanced at me when I came in. He seemed a bit preoccupied, so I sat on a hay bale behind him, leaning my back against the wall, listening to his steady stream of curses. In between the four-letter words and uniquely regional phrases, I gathered that some of the gears had jammed together at an odd angle and he was having trouble removing the clutch assembly from the housing. I was learning a lot, listening to him muttering, about the finer points of motorcycle mechanics and the sex life of small waterfowl.

The barn door slid open with a crash. I heard footsteps slamming through the hay and Meri appeared in the doorway. She stood with a shotgun cradled in the crook of her arm. I felt my jaw drop and I started to ask her what was going on, but the look on her face made me freeze. Her face was flushed a mottled red and held so tight that her bones showed through, all angles and planes. She never even glanced at me, only stood there, tension zinging through her body, staring at Taylor with her mouth set in a hard, fierce line.

"Why are you here?" she asked. Her tone was cutting and cruel.

Taylor jumped up from the hay faster than if someone had

kicked him. He stumbled backward until he bumped against the far wall. He pressed himself against it, stood staring at Meri, his eyes moving down to the gun, and then back up again to her face. His tan faded to pale except for the two bright spots high on his cheeks.

"Aunt Beatrice sent me," he said, his voice dropping an octave. "She said you had a guest with a broken bike."

Meri lifted the barrel of the gun so that it wavered somewhere near his feet. "The woods are full of mechanics around here. Why would she send you?"

Taylor's boots twitched like he was afraid for his toes. "Aunt Beatrice said it would be a good opportunity for us to talk things out since you don't come into town for any of the shindigs anymore."

Meri's face twisted, and the gun barrel rose to point at his knees. "Get out of my barn," she said in a voice that made my skin prickle. I stood and tried to catch her eyes, but she never took them off Taylor.

He gestured, with a slight jerk of his hand, at the tools and bike parts lying in the hay. "Aunt Beatrice said that maybe if I did something to help you that you might be more inclined to forgive me."

Meri's face turned colder than winter, the barrel rose and pointed at his chest. "Have you told her what you did?"

Taylor put a hand over his heart and shook his head, his eyes going wide and white. "I've never told anybody, Meri. Honest, I haven't," he said. The bright spots on his cheeks grew and spread down his neck. "You've never told anyone either."

Meri's eyes narrowed. "Who was there to tell? Everyone I loved was gone."

"You could've told Aunt Beatrice," Taylor said softly.

"And would she have believed me if I did, golden boy?"

Taylor rubbed at his chest. "No. I mean, probably not." He reached up with a slow hand and took off his cap. He rolled the brim into tight tube as he dug a toe down into the hay. "I'm sorry,

Meri. I truly am. I would take it all back if I could. I would make it right if I knew how. You just tell me what to do and I'll do it."

The barrel held steady at his chest. "Nothing you do now can fix what you broke."

"I know that," he said. "I was just hoping that maybe we could talk or something."

"I have nothing to say to you and I don't want you here." Meri's hands tightened around the stock. I could see the tendons standing out on the backs of them. "My mom and my dad wouldn't want you here, either."

Taylor's chin dimpled and began to quiver. He unrolled his cap and put it on, pulling the sharply curved brim low over his eyes. He took a careful step forward and, moving slowly, he bent to pack his tools. Meri stared at him. The contempt pouring out of her was so strong that it was uncomfortable standing near her. She kept the gun pointed at Taylor. Her finger wasn't on the trigger, but it kept inching nearer to it. I backed away from her, not sure what was scaring me more, that Taylor had a gun pointing at his head or the expression on Meri's face.

Taylor left a line of tools lying in the hay. He glanced up at me. "These are the tools you're going to need. I'll leave them here for you. If you follow the assembly pattern on the instruction page you should be all right." He snapped the lid of his toolbox. "Maybe on your way out of town you can drop the tools off at my garage." Taylor grabbed the box and stood slowly. He turned his head toward Meri, but his eyes were still on the ground. "I'll leave now if you're not going to shoot me."

Meri raised the gun and pointed it at his face. Taylor winced. She raised it higher, laid the barrel back against her shoulder and stepped out of the doorway.

He walked to the door and brushed by Meri, who shifted to avoid touching him. He stopped just outside and turned. "Meri, I truly am sorry for all the things that happened. I still think we could make a go of it, in spite of everything. We could be good for each other."

"It would be good only for you, Taylor." Meri's words were clipped and precise.

Taylor frowned at that but then just nodded. He walked out of the barn, and I stepped out of the stall. Meri lowered the gun and set it against the wall. I watched her while we listened to the truck door screech and slam. She was staring at nothing, her spine rigid and straight.

The truck engine turned over with a soft purr. We both stood still and listened as the sound of crunching tires faded into silence. Meri slumped against the door jam. She buried her face in her hands and sank to her knees, her shoulders shaking violently. I stood over her fidgeting, not knowing what to do. I didn't understand what had just happened. She made a ragged gasping sound. I knelt down beside her and put my hand on her shoulder. She leaned sidewise into me, and I held her, rocking her gently, stroking her hair, but my eyes kept flicking to the gun.

Night was falling and we were still sitting in the throughway on the barn floor, our backs against the rough planked wall. Meri was leaning against me with her head on my shoulder and her arm tucked around my waist, our legs outstretched and tangled. She had not said a word in over an hour. I held on to her, stroking her shoulder, not knowing what else to do, not knowing if I should speak or not. The crickets that lived in the dark corners of the barn started their chirping.

I was out of my depth, uncomfortable and confused. The curve of her shoulder was so familiar to me now, its strength and expressions. I could read her body and understand what it was telling me, but sitting there in the near dark, inches away from a loaded shotgun, it occurred to me that I didn't really know much about her. She knew a great deal about me. Once I started talking, it was hard to get me to stop, but she only talked about the things that surrounded us, the farm, the house, the weather. She didn't talk much about herself. I assumed that, being raised in a small town, there hadn't been much to talk about, outside of what happened to her parents, and she didn't seem ready to talk about that. Clearly, I'd made a dumb assumption, maybe even a dangerous one.

I heard hoofbeats thudding dully over the grass. Sergeant came into the barn through the pasture door. He walked up to us, put his head down and snuffed in Meri's hair. She reached out blindly. Her hand found his nose and he huffed into it. Meri shuddered slightly. Her eyes focused and seemed to come back alive.

"I guess he's looking for his dinner." She sounded flat and hollow.

"Doesn't he eat grass?" I asked. "He's got dinner everywhere."

Sergeant jerked his head and hit my chin with his nose.

"Hey!" I rubbed my chin and glared at him. He chuffed a wet breath into my face. I guessed it was an apology of a sort. I took it that way anyway and lifted a hand to rub underneath his jaw.

Meri stared at us. There was still something in her face that made me nervous, something unfamiliar and out of place.

"I didn't realize it had gotten so late," she said. "I'd better get Sergeant his oats."

She untangled herself from me and stood slowly as if her whole body was sore. It probably was. My bones creaked when I tried to stand and my butt felt numb. She took hold of Sergeant's bridle and led him over to his stall. I watched her as she dished out a small measure of feed, changed his water and began to brush him lightly while he munched and stamped. Her face was thin and drawn, chin tucked in, her mouth turned down severely at the corners. It was an expression I'd never seen on her before. It was cruel and cold, like the promise of bad things coming. I didn't like it, but I hadn't put it there and I didn't know how to take it off.

She stopped brushing in mid-stroke and leaned against Sergeant's flank. He flicked his tail, and it swished against her. I stepped inside the stall and stood behind her, lifting my hand to touch her but dropping it again before I did.

"Meri, tell me what I can do to help."

"That's the same thing Taylor asked." It was the winter voice, cold and filled with jagged ice.

It scared me. "Are you going to point a gun at my head?"

"Do I need to?" She turned around. Her eyes were dark in the failing light, intense and frightening.

The brush fell from her fingers and dropped into the hay. The skin on Sergeant's flanks rippled and shivered. "I want to kill him, Bea," she said in a voice as empty as dark. "I want to pull the trigger so bad it makes my hands hurt."

That made me take a step back. The way she looked reminded me of something big and scary, and then I remembered where I had seen eyes like hers were now. The two men at the Texas diner had eyes like that and voices just as dead. I knew what they were and what they would've done to me if I hadn't seen them first. I never expected to see that threat in Meri's eyes. Fear tickled along my spine, and I started to back away from her.

"No, Bea. Don't," she said, her hands reaching for me. I shied away from her touch, stumbling, slamming my shoulder against the wall. She stared at me, crouched and shivering, and her face crumpled. "I would never hurt you, Bea. Not you." She held her hands curled in front of her as if something horrible was resting in her palms.

"How can I believe that?"

She closed her hands into tight fists and then opened them again. She rubbed them hard against her jeans. "You don't understand."

"No, I don't. I don't understand you at all right now." And I wondered if I ever had. I'd been quick to trust because her life seemed so uncomplicated and everything she said rang true. I never thought to listen for the things she wasn't saying. I had missed something. Something scary. I was so tired of being scared. It made me angry.

Sergeant tossed his head and stamped a hind foot. Meri stuffed her hands into her pockets. Her eyes were still dark, but she seemed less threatening postured like that.

"I think you need to explain this to me, Meri," I said, letting the anger leak into my voice. I forced my knees to straighten, my shoulders to square, but I stayed pressed against the wall. "What have I walked into? Is this some kind of a feud? A Hatfield and McCoy kind of thing?"

She shook her head and took her hands out of her pockets slowly, turning them palm up. They were empty. She held them out to me.

I folded my arms across my chest. "You need to tell me who else is out there that you want to kill or that wants to kill you."

She dropped her hands. "It's not a feud, Bea, and there's nobody out there that I really want to kill. Not even Taylor. Not really. Maybe." She shrugged. "Well, I didn't, anyway."

"If I wasn't here would you have shot him?"

"If you weren't here, he wouldn't have come over."

"That's not a real answer."

Her mouth opened and closed. She looked around the barn and then back at Sergeant, done with the oats, picking at his hay. She shook her head. "I don't know, Bea."

That was a real answer, an honest answer, and it made me feel a little less angry and a lot less scared. Whatever hate lived inside her, if it was an honest hate, it could be reasoned with.

"Okay, so tell me what this is about."

She turned slightly and rubbed a hand across Sergeant's shoulder. He arched his neck and swished his tail. "It's a very long story." Meri fingered the braids I had worked into his mane. "I'll tell it to you, but can we go back to the house first?"

"Yes, I think we should." It would be better to hear about this thing in the bright lights of the kitchen and not in the cold dark of the barn.

She smiled softly at me, and the Meri I loved slowly crawled back into her face. It was an effort not to return the smile, but I wasn't quite done being angry. She stepped past me, as gingerly as Taylor had stepped past her, as she walked out of the stall. I stepped out behind her. She stood very still with her hands at her sides. Her expression was cautious, wary and waiting.

I took a deep breath, breathing in the smells of the barn, horses and hay, pine and old leather. And the scent of lemon dish soap. I let some of the anger go. I don't know how long I could've held on to it anyway with her standing there like that, waiting for me to say something.

"I'll make dinner if you don't mind having something from the freezer."

Her eyes softened and her shoulders fell just a bit. "I'm not *that* hungry," she said.

I huffed at her. "My cooking's not that bad."

Meri smiled gently. We both knew it was. She turned to shut the bottom door to Sergeant's stall and stood looking in at him. Her expression turned wistful and sad. "Sergeant was my mom's horse, you know. She used to braid his hair like that, twisting in ribbons and things."

"No, I didn't know that." I looked over her shoulder at Sergeant who was standing there with his head bowed, eyes blinking slowly, a small straw of hay hanging from the corner of his mouth. "I'm beginning to see just how much I don't know. That frightens me, Meri."

She turned around and stretched out her hand to me again. I looked at it and then over at the gun still leaning against the wall. Meri dropped her hand. She picked up the gun and went to put it in the tack room. When she came out, she closed the door behind her, jiggling the handle to show me that it was locked. She held her hand out to me, again.

"Please," she said. Her voice was warm again and soft with just a shade of longing.

I slipped my hand into hers, and some of the tightness left her face.

"Thank you," she whispered as her fingers closed around

mine.

We walked out of the barn and she shut the door behind us.

The smell of roasting potatoes wafted out from the oven. Greens were boiling on the stove, and I was doing my usual job of chopping and dicing for the salad. I was still trying to learn my way around the kitchen so I could do my fair share, but it usually ended in some kind of disaster. Meri truly didn't like my attempts at re-creating the dishes I was familiar with. It was too fancy with the spices, she said. Her nose always wrinkled at the smell of rosemary and basil unless it was in spaghetti, which I hated. She made extravagant breakfasts with shaved cinnamon and orange zest, but for her dinners, she was strictly a-salt-and-pepper girl, maybe some garlic if she felt adventuresome. Her meals were simple and straightforward, meat and a vegetable or three, rolls or biscuits on the side. At first, it was a welcome change from long and elaborate many-coursed affairs, but after a while, I found myself longing for something other than beef or chicken. Like duck or salmon, maybe, a salad made of something other than romaine lettuce, and a three-tiered dessert of something decadently chocolate instead of vanilla pudding from a plastic cup.

I was fantasizing about a cold artichoke salad as I sliced carrots at an oblique angle and made little star shapes out of the cucumbers. I'm sure Meri would have let me borrow the truck if I really had to have something different, but I was still too afraid to go into town. Meri did all the grocery shopping, and I wasn't in a position to complain about what she fed me. She peered over my shoulder at the florets of cherry tomatoes and rolled her eyes. I stuck my tongue out at her and she snapped a kitchen towel at my butt. She missed. I tossed the salad together and put the bowl on the table.

"What would you like to drink?" I asked her, heading for the refrigerator.

Meri leaned over the sink and drained the water out of the greens. "I think I'd like a beer." Steam from the pan rose and swirled around her head. "I don't suppose you drink beer, but there's plenty in there if you want one."

I got out a beer for her and one for myself. She was right, though. I didn't drink beer. Or I never had. Not because of any snobbery, but just because it was never offered. Not even here. The bottles were always in the refrigerator, but I'd never seen Meri drink one. I assumed they were for guests and visitors.

"Am I supposed to set these on the table," I asked "or should I pour the beer into a glass first?"

She stopped to look at me, a plate of baked chicken steaming in her hands. "Is that a joke or a serious question?"

"Serious question. My upbringing was a little deficient in beer etiquette."

She nodded very slowly, as if she was trying to come to terms with that. She got a funny look on her face, one eyebrow raised and the other eye squinted half closed, but I couldn't tell if she was distressed or amused. "You'd better just set the bottles on the table," she said at last. "There's a bit of a trick to pouring beer into a glass. The bottle opener is in the drawer by the fridge."

I rummaged through the drawer, found the opener and pulled the tops off the bottles. They came off with a pop and a whoosh. Little wisps of beer vapor floated up the necks. It was pretty, but it smelled strange, sort of like sourdough bread. I set the bottles on the table and sat. Meri had already served a plate for me, heavy on the salad, and was making her own, heavier on the potatoes. I took a sip of the beer. It was bitter and foamed across my tongue. It tickled my nose and didn't taste at all like it smelled. Meri was watching me.

"Not bad," I said through stiffly puckered lips and set the bottle down.

Meri shook her head and got up from the table. She poured a glass of water and set it in front of me before she settled in her chair. She seemed a little disappointed.

"There are some really good vineyards around here," she said. "They give tours and do tasting parties and stuff like that. We can go to some, if you want, or if you tell me what you like, I can pick something out for you."

"I don't suppose you drink wine," I said.

Meri shook her head. "I've never found one that I liked very much. They're either too sweet, too sour or they taste like the inside of the barrel." She fiddled with her fork, poking it at her potatoes. "Your life has been very different than mine, Bea." She set her fork down and picked up her beer. "Do you think we're just too different?"

I laid my fork across my plate. "I didn't think so yesterday, but today, how can I tell? I don't really know anything about you."

She gestured at the walls around us. "This is what I am, Bea. This house. This land. You can see me here and know all the important things there are to know." She set the bottle on the table and tucked her hands into her lap. "And you know you love me. I think. Do you still love me?"

"Yes." I was surprised that I didn't have to think about it. It was true that she scared me a little now, but it didn't diminish the love. I had no idea why not. It should have, but it just didn't.

She smiled a little. "You know I love you. What else is there worth knowing?"

"Everything," I said sharply. "You've been keeping things from me, Meri, big important things. It makes me wonder what else you're hiding. What else is there in your life that might jump out at me and say 'boo'?"

Meri stared her bottle. "I only have one ghost in my closet," she said studying the label closely.

"Taylor," I said.

"Taylor." She nodded slowly and then slumped down in her chair. "I was born in this house. Except for college, I've never lived anywhere else but here. I know every single person in this town, at least by reputation." Her face got that pinched look I hated so much, full of pain and anger, suspicion and sadness. "Taylor and

I were practically raised together. We played the same games, went to the same school, rode the same bus. We started dating in high school and were inseparable until our senior year."

"What happened in your senior year?"

"Nothing," she said looking down at her lap, "but it was a lot of nothing."

I scooted my chair back from the table just a little. I wasn't trying to distance myself from her. I was only trying to prepare myself for what I thought was coming. "Was it ever serious between you two?"

She started to shrug, but her shoulders fell before they rose very far. "Everyone assumed we would marry. I did too, at first. I even slept with him a few times. Prom night, graduation, stuff like that. You know, all the times you're expected to, but I didn't care for it. I did it, but I never wanted to. It wasn't what the books said it should be. It wasn't like what it was in the movies. I kept trying to feel something special, but I never did. I figured the books were all lying and feelings like that didn't exist."

So far, I understood exactly what she was saying. I spent my early teens wondering what was wrong with me that I wasn't giddy over all the boys. I didn't want what the other girls seemed to want. I couldn't even imagine wanting it, but I got very good at pretending that I did.

Meri picked up her beer, cradling it in her hands. "When I went to college, I met this girl. Red hair and freckles. We were both English majors so we were in a lot of the same classes. We got together to study a lot. She liked arguing, and I had plenty of things to argue about. I liked her. She said that the way I talked was cute." Meri looked up at me. "Do you think the way I talk is cute?"

I shrugged. I hadn't thought about her accent in while. "When I first heard you talk, I thought you used too many vowels. Now, I don't notice it so much."

Meri frowned. That probably wasn't the answer she wanted. "Well, she thought it was cute." She tapped the bottom of the bottle on the table. "One time I was sitting next to her on the couch in her dorm trying to explain why I thought Hemmingway was a lazy writer, and right out of the blue, she leaned over and kissed me." Meri shook her head, remembering. "I was so stunned, I just sat there, like a bump on a log. Then she did it again, but that time I kissed her back. Inside that kiss was everything the books were talking about, fireworks, bells, electricity, everything. It really did exist. I'd just been looking for it in the wrong place."

I looked down at my plate of slowly wilting lettuce. I didn't like the picture of Meri kissing someone else. "What happened to her?" I asked. "Where is she now?"

Meri took a hefty swig from her bottle and set it on the table. "I don't know. She was from a city where people like us weren't a big deal. She wanted to be open about everything. She wanted to go out on dates and to go to dances and hold hands in the park. She wanted to come home with me and meet my parents." She scratched at the label, peeling one corner and smoothing it down again. "It scared me. In this town, the word 'gay' still means happy and 'lesbian' isn't even in the dictionary. I wasn't ready to challenge my upbringing. I couldn't be as open as she wanted me to be, so she found somebody else who could."

In a way, I knew what that was like, too. People in my own life always seemed to want me to be something I wasn't and they made it very clear that what I was wasn't an acceptable thing to be. It made me afraid of myself, afraid that I might do something that betrayed my real feelings and everyone would know how perverted I was and then they would do bad things in order to "fix" me.

"I'm sorry," I said. "That must have hurt."

Meri lifted her beer and drank. She touched her mouth with back of her hand. "It did. But what was I going to do?"

"What did you do?" I asked with just the hint of a smile. I did know her at least that well.

Meri smiled thinly and drank the last of her beer in two quick gulps. She looked over at mine. I shoved it across the table and

73

she picked it up, holding it in her hands, rubbing the dew off the glass with her thumb.

"I came home from college the summer before my senior year and announced to my parents that I was gay, not as in happy." She raised the bottle to her lips but lowered it again without taking a sip. "It wasn't really that bad. They were upset, naturally. They had their own dreams of what they thought my life would be like. They assumed that I would come home from college, work a little and then marry Taylor. They figured I would settle someplace nearby"—she waved the bottle at the wall—"have a couple of kids, support them in their old age and eventually inherit the farm. It was a nice dream, and I didn't object to it except for the part about marrying Taylor. My parents and I had some sharp words, but I never doubted that they loved me."

Meri's grip tightened on the bottle, her knuckles going white as she tucked it against her chest. "Right before I was supposed to go back to school, I told Taylor that I wouldn't marry him. He didn't take it very well, especially since I couldn't tell him why. He was very, very angry. We said some nasty things to each other. He said them first, but I made sure I had the ugliest last word I could think of. Then he hit me." Meri punched with the bottle. Beer sloshed out and splattered her hand. She ignored the drops as they ran down her wrists and dripped onto the floor. "My dad found out. He could hardly help it since I had a huge bruise under my eye." She touched her left cheek with her fingertips. "The next day, my dad went into to town and beat the stuffing out of Taylor, broke some teeth, bloodied his nose and told him not to ever set foot on the farm again."

I smiled grimly. I could appreciate her story even if I didn't understand it. My father would have told me that the black eye was my fault, punished me for marring the family image and then sued the boy just for the hell of it. "Your dad sounds like a wonderful man," I said.

"He was the best dad in the whole world." Meri wiped at her eyes with the back of her hand leaving a smear of beer across her cheek. She laughed a short, sad sound. "Mom told me that if dad hadn't done it, she would have beat the crap out of Taylor herself. She would have, too. She was such a strong woman, not very tall, but full of fire."

I nodded, though again, I didn't really understand. I didn't know any strong women, except Meri. My mother was so non-descript and such a vague part of my life that I had trouble even remembering what she looked like. She spoke seldom and almost never to me. My father, and her father before him, had beaten her down, well and truly, long before I was ever born. "I wish I could have met your parents," I said.

"I wish you could have, too." Meri set the beer bottle on the table and hugged her arms across her chest. "It's still hard to talk about it."

"Have you ever talked to anybody about it?"

She shook her head.

"There was nobody to talk to," I guessed.

"There was nobody left."

Meri got up from the table and began to pace around the kitchen, her body a chaos of conflicting signals. The dip of her head was sad, the tight set of her shoulders angry, her footsteps stumbling and confused. She had her hands buried deep inside her pockets.

"Taylor never got over it," she said, "me or the beating my father gave him."

"I heard him say that he still thinks you would be good for each other."

Meri froze in mid-stride. "Goddamn arrogant son of bitch," she said through clenched teeth. Her face crumpled, and she collapsed back into her chair. "He took everything away from me, Bea, my parents, my dreams, my future. How could I not want to hurt him?"

"Tell me the story, Meri. Help me understand it."

Meri scrubbed at her face with her hands. "The summer after graduation, I came home to stay for a while, partly to decide what

I wanted to do with my life, and partly to put off the deciding." She dropped her hands. Her eyes were glittering brightly. "I met Taylor in town one day. He cornered me in the produce section of Twiggy's grocery store. He said how sorry he was for hitting me, swore he'd never do it again and begged me to change my mind about marrying him. He got down on his knees, right there in front of God and everybody, in between two bushels of green beans and a pyramid of tomatoes." Meri's face paled and then flushed. "I said some harsh things and then turned around and left him kneeling there. I hadn't forgotten what that punch felt like." Meri's face paled again, her color fading almost to gray.

"Meri," I said, "you don't have to tell me any more. I think I understand enough."

She shook her head fiercely. "You don't understand anything."

I stood and moved around the table to sit in the chair next to hers. I put my arms around her shoulders. They were trembling, and she leaned into me. She took a deep breath and let it out slowly. Maybe she was counting to ten or something, but whatever it was, some of the color came back into her cheeks.

"Okay," I said pressing my knee against hers. "I'm ready to understand. What did Taylor do?"

She shifted in her chair. "That night, after the grocery store thing, Taylor snuck up to the house and put a very large king snake inside the farm truck."

My hand stilled against her shoulder. That wasn't what I was expecting to hear. It wasn't even a close second. "A snake?" I asked. I wasn't particularly fond of snakes, and it certainly wasn't a nice thing for Taylor to do, but I couldn't see why Meri would want to kill him over it. Meri shook her head at my confusion. Her eyes focused on the dripping beer bottle making wet rings on the table.

"It was just a joke," she said. "A mean and ugly joke, but he didn't mean me any harm. It wasn't a poisonous snake or anything. He just wanted to scare me, and he knew that I did most of the farm chores. We kept sheep then, and I had to drive out to the west pasture every morning to count heads and make sure they were all right." She paused and then she leaned harder into me. "I guess he imagined that I would open the truck door and the snake would pop out. I would run screaming and he would get the last laugh." Meri squeezed her eyes shut. "I wouldn't have, though. I wouldn't have screamed." I gripped her shoulder tighter. I believed her.

"But that morning, before I woke up, Dad decided to take the truck over to the next town to buy some feed for the chickens. Mom decided to go with him to do some shopping at one of the fancy stores." Meri started to tremble, her shoulder shivering under my hand. "You have to cross the mountains to get there," she said softly. "They're not big mountains as mountains go, but there are some steep parts and some tight turns."

I remembered those tight turns, on the motorcycle, in the rain. I remembered the steep parts too, the dark trees and the small points of light far below. "What happened, Meri?"

"Somewhere on the way back, my father lost control of the truck. It crashed through a guardrail and went over the side. The truck rolled over so many times that it didn't look like a truck anymore. I made Jeremy, our sheriff, show me the pictures." Her eyes opened wide. "My mom had bought a new dress. They found it on the slope about halfway down the mountain. It was still in the bag, still on its hanger."

"Was it the snake?" I asked, hushed and horrified.

"They found what was left of it in the cab afterward, twisted around the brake pedal." Meri shuddered and stilled. "My dad was terrified of snakes." She turned her head. Her eyes were haunted and hollow. "Taylor stayed dead drunk for almost a month. It was pretty clear to me that he knew something he wasn't saying, and I had a good idea of what that something might be. I ran him to ground, put the shotgun to his head and made him tell me everything."

I blinked at her. Her eyes had gone scary again, her voice cold and dark, but this time it didn't scare me quite as much. This time I understood a little. "It's a wonder that you didn't pull the trigger," I said quietly.

"I did." She leaned her head back until it was resting against my arm, her eyes staring into the middle distance. "I didn't know much about guns then. I didn't know my father stored them unloaded. I pulled the trigger and the stupid thing just clicked. I kept pulling and it just kept clicking until Taylor pissed himself and passed out."

"Today, in the barn, was that the same gun?"

Meri nodded, her hair rubbing against my arm. "It was the only one I kept."

"Was it loaded?"

Meri nodded again. "Both barrels."

"But you didn't pull the trigger this time."

"No, I didn't." She rolled her head over to look at me. "Do I get points for that?"

"This is not something you should joke about, Meri. You very nearly killed someone today."

"Not quite so near as you're thinking."

"What do you mean?"

"The safety was on. If I had pulled the trigger, nothing would've happened. It wouldn't have even clicked."

"I don't understand what you're saying, Meri."

Meri's eyes searched mine for a long time. "Right after my parents died, my only thought was to hunt Taylor down and kill him. First him and then me. Today, I'm not so ready to die." She sighed lightly. "I guess that makes me less ready to deal out death to others."

The kitchen light was harsh to her upturned face. Lines that had no business being there creased the sides of her mouth, furrowed across her brow. I pulled her closer to me.

"I might be willing to give you a few points for that."

She raised an eyebrow. "I thought we weren't going to joke about this."

"I'm not joking."

Meri sat up in her chair, leaned forward and reached for the beer. She drank deeply and wiped her mouth on her sleeve. "The hell of it all is that Taylor reminds me of my dad. He looks a lot like him and talks like him, but he's not really anything like him at all. It's like he's only a shadow of him, a bad counterfeit." She finished the beer with a few quick swallows and set the empty bottle on the table next to the other one.

"I'm sorry I scared you, Bea. I'm sorry if I'm not the person you thought I was," she said with a hollowness that wasn't at all empty, but filled with shades of love and loss. "I know you said you still love me, but I'll understand if you don't want to stay here anymore."

I reached out to rub slow circles across the small of her back. "Remember when you first found me in the barn? You said I looked pretty scary wearing all that blood and leather."

She smiled a little. "Yeah, you did look a fright."

"But I didn't turn out to be what you thought I was."

"Bea," she said dryly, "I thought you were an escaped convict."

"But you still helped me when I asked you to."

"You were hurt."

"You're hurt now."

She shifted in her chair. "Yeah, I guess so."

She got up, went over to the refrigerator and opened the door. I followed her. I took her hand off the handle and shut the door before she could reach in for another beer. She frowned as I touched her cheek.

"There are less destructive ways to deal with what hurts you."

"Such as?"

I let my fingers fall, trailing down her throat, dipped them inside the open collar of her shirt and traced over the line of her collarbone. She closed her eyes and lifted her chin. I leaned over and kissed the spot where her jaw met her neck and started unbuttoning her shirt, letting my knuckles rub against her skin with each button undone. She made a little mewing sound when I pulled the shirt open and unbuttoned her jeans. She slipped her hands around my waist, pulling me to her. I kissed her mouth, drinking deeply of the sour beer taste that coated her tongue. Her breath came warm and fast against my cheek, her hands kneading my hips. She pulled away suddenly. Her hands slipped around to my front and fumbled with the buttons on my shirt, but they all pulled and stuck. She snarled and yanked. Two of the buttons popped off and hit the floor with tiny clicking bounces. She gave up on the buttons and lifted the shirt over my head. She tore her own shirt off and then struggled out of her bra. When I slipped my bra off too she stood still for a second looking at me with a ferocious hunger that all by itself was just this side of scary. She crushed me against her, her face buried against my neck, teeth nipping, hands rubbing hot over my skin.

"Upstairs?" I asked. My voice sounded low and rough.

"No," she whispered. "Right here, right now."

We sank to the floor. The tile was cold against my skin. Meri slipped her legs between mine and spread my knees with hers. She knelt over me, her hands kneading, pressing, pinching, caressing, her mouth kissing, tongue licking, teeth biting until I was twisting and squirming underneath her, moaning with low ragged groans. I caught her off balance and pulled her down on top of me, crushing her breasts against mine. I wrapped my legs around hers and pinned her tight. We became all fervent lips and probing tongues, grasping hands and deep-throated moans. She held on to my hips and ground herself into me, blue jeans rubbing hard and fast, almost to the point of pain, our breath coming in short quick gasps.

"Oh god, oh fuck, oh god," Meri whispered.

A short, sharp spasm shuddered through me and I reached to cup her butt, pressing her harder into me. My hips arched off the floor.

The kitchen door opened. My body sank and stilled.

Meri didn't hear it.

"Stop, Meri," I whispered harshly as I pushed her shoulders away from me. "Meri, stop."

She pulled herself up and looked down at me, her face a mix of confusion and concern. "What?" she asked still breathing hard and ragged. "What's wrong? Was I hurting you?"

I shook my head and jerked my chin over her shoulder. She raised her head and froze. I twisted to see who it was. There was a little old lady standing in the doorway. She was a round roly-poly woman in a pink cardigan sweater with bright blue hair, shock and disgust dancing all over her face.

"Hi, Auntie Bea," Meri said in a small, thin voice.

The little old lady spun on her heels and slammed the door shut behind her.

"Oh, shit," Meri said and collapsed on top of me.

Meri drank quite a bit after Aunt Beatrice left, and I didn't try to stop her again. After the beer ran out, I put her to bed, made sure she was sleeping on her side, and lay down next to her. I had my arms tucked behind my head as I listened to her snore and to the creaking of the house as the night dragged on and on. In the morning, she took a long time in the shower. I stayed in bed listening to the rush of water and the groans of the old water pipes. Usually, she sang or hummed as she washed. Today she was silent. I reached under the sheets, slipped a hand under my shorts and touched myself gently. My pubic bone was sore, but inside I felt haunted and hungry. There was an aching emptiness that still wanted Meri to fill it, so I lay there waiting for her to finish in the bathroom, waiting for her to come back to me.

Meri dropped something in the shower that bounced around with dull thuds. She cursed and the water turned off. I waited for another ten minutes, staring at the bathroom door, slowly combing my fingers through my hair. The hair dryer turned on and I got tired of waiting. I got out of bed, slipped on yesterday's clothes and went out to the barn.

I measured out Sergeant's breakfast and watched him eat, gave him a quick brush, checked his hooves and turned him out for the day. He didn't go far. He leaned his head in through the pasture window to watch me rake the old wet straw out of his stall. I dumped it and came back to spread new straw around. Sergeant was still peeking in the window, and I stopped to pat his neck. He nudged me with his nose.

"What is it, Sarge?" I asked him. "You want me to leave?"

"No," Meri answered for him, "he's telling you that there's someone behind you."

I turned around. Meri wasn't wearing blue jeans. She was in a frilly blouse and a pleated skirt. She had makeup on, inexpertly done. The blush made her face look pale, and the heavy mascara made the dark circles under her eyes look darker. I could have helped her with the makeup if she had asked, but maybe she didn't want any more of my help. I leaned the rake against the wall. "All that for Aunt Beatrice?"

"She's my closest living relative," Meri said as she smoothed her skirt flat against her thighs, "my father's older sister. She's all that I have left of my immediate family."

"You look nice," I said dully.

Meri flushed. "It's not very fashionable or anything." It wasn't and she seemed uncomfortable in it. She was stiff and wooden as if she was lost and out of place standing there in the hay in her skirt and heels.

I smiled and shrugged. "The classic stuff never goes out of style."

She smiled nervously.

I pointed at her feet. "It's probably not a good idea to be walking through the barn in those shoes." I held my hand out to her. "Come on, I'll walk you to the truck."

She looked at my hand. Her face was drawn and pale, her eyes colorless.

"All right," I said, dropping my hand, "it's okay. I

understand."

"Do you?"

"Sure." I shrugged with what I hoped was nonchalance. "This is a small town and your aunt likes to talk. You want us to cool off for a while, and I should act more like a real guest if people come over."

Meri's face fell. That wasn't the right answer. "It's too late for that, I think." Her hands hung at her sides like she didn't know what to do with them with no pockets in her skirt to stuff them into.

Sergeant snorted from the window. I felt like snorting too. "What do you want, then?"

"I can't lose any more of my family." Her voice sounded small and soft. "If my aunt disowns me then all of my cousins will too. I can't let that happen. I need them."

A spark of anger flickered inside me. "Oh, right," I said, folding my arms across my chest, "and we've been seeing so much of them lately."

Hurt filled her eyes. "Sarcasm isn't going to help things, Bea."

"What will?" My tone sounded cold even to me.

Her hands clenched and unclenched. She opened them flat and rubbed her palms against her skirt. I clenched my teeth together hard and promised myself that I was not going to cry.

"Do you want me to leave?" I lifted my chin with maybe just a small touch of challenge.

Meri hugged her arms across her stomach. "Maybe that would be best, but only for a little while, just until this blows over."

That was not the answer I was expecting. It hit me square in the chest. "This isn't going to blow over." My words came out much harsher than I meant them to, but my throat had tightened almost to closing.

"You don't know that." Meri's own anger sparked in her eyes. "Maybe it will blow over if I can think of something good enough to tell Aunt Beatrice."

"What's there to tell her? She saw you fucking a woman on your kitchen floor. How are you going to explain that?"

Meri's eyes widened and she blinked a few times. "I wouldn't exactly call it fucking. We still had our pants on."

"That's just great, Meri," I said, putting my hands on my hips. "That'll explain everything. You can tell her that we weren't doing what it looked like we were doing because we still had our pants on. I'm sure she'll be convinced."

"I'm not going to say that, Bea." Meri's hands twitched against her legs. "I'm not even sure what we were doing. Everything happened so fast."

So much for my promises. I was going to cry. "Weren't we making love?"

"I don't know," she said. "I don't know anything."

"What are you going to call it when you talk to her?" I swiped at my cheek with an angry hand. "A lapse in judgment? A momentary indiscretion? CPR administered in a unique and unusual way?"

"Bea, please don't do this," Meri said, raising her hands to rub at her temples.

"Oh, I've got it. Why don't you tell her that I was a bad influence on you? Tell her I came breezing in here with my big city ideas and seduced you, but you have seen the error of your ways and have decided to marry Taylor after all and will raise a whole litter of children just to prove that you've repented."

"That's cruel, Bea." Meri's hands dropped again to her side.

"No, Meri, it isn't. It's reality. That will be the price of her forgiveness. I've been there before."

"What do you mean?"

I gave her a smile that made her frown. "My father. That was the price he demanded of me. I was to marry and give him his grandchildren. That's what it cost to be his daughter. That's what it's going to cost you to be Aunt Bea's niece. If you go over there begging forgiveness, she'll insist that you 'do the right thing.'"

Meri's shoulders stiffened. "I won't marry Taylor."

"It won't matter who you marry, just so long as you get married."

Meri threw her hands in the air. "What am I supposed to do then, Bea? I don't have a motorcycle. I can't run away from here. Everything I am is tied to this land, to this town, to these people."

That made me stop and think. It was true. She didn't have the same options I did. She didn't really have any options at all, but I wasn't sure she could see that. "You have to decide," I said.

"Decide what?"

"Whether to live the truth and risk being lonely or live a lie surrounded by your kin."

"I'm not you, Bea." Meri shook her head slowly. "I need my family. I need to know that they're close by."

"I'm close by," I said softly.

"For how long?" Meri stared at me, seeing I don't know what in my face, but her expression softened. "Do you see?" she asked. "No matter what I do, you'll leave anyway, and then I'll be more alone than I ever was before."

I didn't know what to say to that. She was right.

"You want me to leave right now?" It was almost a whisper.

"No, not at all." She started to stretch her hand out but then dropped it again. "I don't want you to leave right now, not right this second."

"But soon."

She didn't answer, and I couldn't bring myself to look at her. I rubbed at the pucker of scar tissue that ran across my forehead.

"The bike's almost fixed," I said. "I can finish in a few days and be out of here before the weekend."

"I didn't mean that soon, either." There was a catch in her voice. Her face was ashen.

I looked around the stall. Sergeant had disappeared from the window. "Why wait?" I asked the question more to myself than to Meri. I drew myself up straighter. My father would say that I was looking down my nose and wouldn't have disapproved in the slightest. "Why wait?"

She opened her mouth and closed it again. I saw her swallow. "When will you come back?"

"I won't, Meri." I raised my chin higher. "You won't even want me too after a while."

"That's not true," she said softly.

I watched a parade of emotions march across her face: hurt, want, loss, fear. It was the fear that stayed, and I thought then that it was true. She wouldn't want me back. I could just picture her getting married, having children, getting religion, locking the memory of me away in an old dark closet in some dusty corner of her heart. She would only think of me on lonely spring nights when the wind turned warm and blew in from the south and she would drink to forget me again. She would shed a tear for the almosts and no one would understand why she did such things. Her life would look so normal, surrounded by kith and kin, but its heart would be a sad one.

It wasn't the direction that I chose, but this choice was hers to make, not mine. "You'd better go see if you can patch things up with your aunt. Soonest started . . ."

". . . is soonest sung," she finished for me.

"I'll get to work on the bike." I brushed past her and went into the next stall. I could still see her through the doorway standing very still, looking at the spot where I had just been. I couldn't tell, now, what she was thinking. From the side, her face seemed closed and hard. She tugged at her skirt and drew herself up. She gave a sharp nod of her head, spun around and walked out of the barn. I heard the truck door creak and slam. The engine turned over with a cough and a splutter. I stood still, my feet rooted in the hay as I listened to the tires crunch over the gravel drive.

The bike stood in front of me, gleaming black, shining chrome and silver duct tape. I lied to Meri. It wouldn't take me a few days to fix it. It only took about an hour and forty-five minutes. I had the right tools, and Taylor had already done all the hard parts. The old clutch assembly came unstuck with a screwdriver and vicious kick. The new assembly came together and slipped right in like it was too scared of me to cause any problems. I connected the pedal and tightened all the bolts. I disconnected the battery charger, coiled the wires and put it back on the shelf in the tack room. I knelt in the hay and replaced the engine guards, fumbling with the screws.

My hands started to shake, but I told myself to stop being an idiot. It would be easier on us both this way. It would be too hard to sleep next to each other in the same bed, both of us knowing that I was going to leave soon. It would be awkward. It would be awful. I dropped the last screw into the hay and couldn't find it again. I didn't really believe myself. Nothing would make leaving any easier. It would only be faster, but sometimes fast is good, like when you're ripping off Band-Aids or breaking your lover's heart. I dug around in the hay looking for the screw for a few minutes, gave up on finding it and went back to the house to take a very long shower. It would be the last one I would enjoy for a while. It was warm enough now to skip the motels. If I could stick to camping grounds, I would be harder to trace. I wondered if Meri would try, and then I wondered how far it was to the Arctic Circle.

My hair was still damp when I pulled the saddlebags out of the cedar chest. For the most part, they were already packed. I never unpacked them except to wash the dirty clothes, which I repacked once they were clean. Everything I wore belonged to Meri: her jeans, her shirts, her sweaters, her socks. Only the underwear was mine and that was only because I couldn't stand her cotton granny drawers. I went to our bedroom and dug my silk underthings out of the drawer she had given to me, the top left hand one of the dresser in her room. She cleared it out for me so I wouldn't have to run through the hallway in a towel, even though I thought she rather liked seeing me in a towel. I folded the jeans and the shirt I'd been wearing and laid them on the end of her bed. Our bed. Her bed again.

My leathers still hung in the closet. They were tighter than I remembered them being and the knee was still torn, but I managed to get everything zipped and tucked. With the saddlebags slung over my shoulder, I headed for the stairs. My boots clomped against the risers as I studied, for the last time, the progression of pictures hanging on the wall. Her mother and father were at the very top of the stairs, young and laughing. A few steps down and a little older, they wore more serious expressions but still had twinkling eyes. Then baby Meri and beaming parents, young Meri, towheaded and pigtailed, an older Meri in cap and gown with mom and dad, grizzle haired, bright eyed and proud.

At the bottom step, there was a picture of me, still with Band-Aids and fading yellow bruises. Sergeant was peering over my shoulder, his upper lip pulled up over his big square teeth. Meri and I fought over that picture. I didn't want it developed, but she did it anyway. After seeing it, I could understand why she wanted to. There was a smile on my face that I hadn't known I owned. One I'd never seen in a magazine or in newspaper print. It was a shining thing, bold and brave, comfortable on my face. I touched my fingers to my scar, still puckered but now not so pink. They both seemed to me to be fitting souvenirs. Meri would have the photograph to remind her of me, and I would have every mirror I would ever look into. I turned away from the stairs, shifted my saddlebags across my shoulders and walked out of the house, across to the barn.

All the system lights across the dash came on when I turned the key. A press of the button, the engine roared and then settled into a tiger's purr. I threw a leg over and kicked up the stand. The engine grumbled impatiently as I rolled the bike slowly out of the barn. I slipped my sunglasses on. My helmet was still lying out in a field somewhere. We never did find it or my gloves. I would have to stop soon and get a new helmet and a new pair of gloves, but for now, I would enjoy the wind in my hair and hope that I wouldn't hit a June bug at seventy. I had enough scars.

My foot tapped the clutch, and it slipped into first gear with a satisfying snick. I nodded my head, revved the engine and started down the drive.

Halfway to the road I saw Meri's truck turning in. She saw me, honked her horn and flicked the lights. My muscles tensed as I swerved off the drive and into the grass. I drove around her without slowing. In the right rearview mirror, I saw her brake lights come on. The truck door opened and Meri jumped out. She was running behind me, awkward and stumbling over the gravel in her heels. I could see her shouting and waving her arms. I flipped the mirror down. It was better this way, I told myself. It was better this way.

I turned onto the road and twisted hard on the throttle. The engine screamed and my front wheel popped off the ground. It fell back again and I picked up speed, the wind rushing past my ears, tires eating the pavement. The green canopy of trees blurred above me. I leaned hard into a curve, my knee just inches from the blacktop, and the driveway, with its little B&B sign of hand-painted letters, disappeared behind me. I pointed my chin at the road and settled into the wind, welcoming the hard press of it against my chest, its harsh fingers scrubbing at my cheeks.

I got lost trying to find Taylor's shop. It wasn't that Laurelvalley was so large, one main street with two rows of three-story buildings and a stop sign at the crossroads, but rather that it was so unremarkable that if you weren't paying attention it would slide right by you. I drove clear through town and out the other side before I realized it. A few wrong turns later and I found myself on a road where the pavement turned to gravel. I was tired of gravel, so I turned around and drove back to the stop sign. There were some kids crossing the street about a block away, boys of nine or ten carrying bamboo fishing poles and one little girl in pigtails carrying the bucket. They stared at me wide-eyed and slack jawed when I rolled to a stop in front of them to ask for directions. Their eyes cut from me to the girl. "It's a lady," one of the boys whispered. The little girl grinned at me, gap toothed and freckled. I smile and gave her the secret-club-for-girls-only head nod. She stood taller and solemnly nodded back to me while the boys just stared. With a dash of luck and a little bit of assertiveness on her part, I didn't think she'd be stuck holding the bucket anymore.

They pointed the way to Taylor's in a mess of garbled confusion, all stumbling over one another, shouting and hopping up and down. I followed the direction that a majority of the little hands were pointing and then found the place anyway, off a side street behind the volunteer fire department and rescue squad. The sign painted neatly on the cinderblock wall read: McNally's Antique Engine Repair, Tool and Die, Welding and Other Fancy Stuff. I might have laughed if I hadn't known about the snake. Nothing Taylor did seemed very funny after that.

I killed the bike, dug the borrowed tools out of the saddlebag and went inside. A large cowbell clanked against the door. The shop was brightly lit and neater than I would have suspected a mechanic's shop to be, though it smelled strongly of gas and stale tobacco. There was a guy leaning over an old long-nosed car, his head buried deep inside the engine. The car looked like a Duesenberg, but I didn't think there were that many left in the world.

"Be with you in a minute," he yelled. There was a clunk and a short stream of cursing that sounded a lot like Taylor. It was. He walked over to me rubbing his head.

"Hey," he said with a wince and a nod. "How's the bike?"

"It's fine," I said. "At least, it shifted okay on the way over." I handed him the tools. "Thanks for letting me borrow these."

He took them from me. "Did you run it through all the gears?" He turned and set the tools on a bench.

I nodded and he smiled.

"You're pretty handy for a girl."

I just stared at him and he coughed into his hand. "Well, then.

90

Do you mind if I take a look at it? Not to check your work," he said quickly when he saw my eyes narrow. "I've never had a good look at a custom before. I'm just curious to see what's different."

I shrugged. He had all day Saturday to see what was different. I knew that wasn't what he wanted, but I was at a point of indecision. Part of me wanted to scream and run away from Laurelvalley as fast as I could go. Another part of me wanted to scream, run to Meri and throw myself at her feet, begging her to let me stay. Letting Taylor look at the bike seemed like a reasonable compromise. He rolled open the big steel door and we went outside. I wheeled the bike into the shop and he clamped it onto the lift. Air hissed and sizzled as it rose. He peered around the engine, played with the clutch and wiggled some hoses. He glanced at me sideways and lifted the torque wrench. I waved him on and he checked to make sure I had set the clutch bolt correctly. The wrench turned and snicked right away.

"You've got the all makings of a good mechanic," he said, grinning at me. "You looking for a job?"

I shook my head. "I'm leaving town."

He looked puzzled and frowned. "I'm sure sorry to hear that. I know you've been a big help to Meri with the chores and all that. Running a farm is a lot of work for just one person." He pulled a dirty rag out of his pocket and wiped a bug speck off the duct tape on the windscreen. He shook the rag out and stuffed it into a different pocket. "Hell, even Sergeant seems to like you. Crazy dumb horse. That's a small miracle, you know. He's never liked anybody but her ever since." A small muscle jumped in his jaw and he turned to the bike.

Ever since her mother died, is what he didn't say. He didn't have to. I'm not even sure he could.

"Are you sure you've got to go, then?" he asked.

"She asked me to leave." It was an effort to keep my voice level and calm, but I think I managed.

He leaned over to fiddle with the air hoses. "I see you turned the clamps around the right way. That's good. It's less of a chance that they'll vibrate loose." He turned around and leaned against the lift. "Not that they would have anyway, but it's better to be safe, right?"

He looked at me sharply, rubbing at his chin with a forefinger. His question wasn't about the air hoses, and I didn't answer him. He shook his head and turned back around.

I rolled my eyes at the back of his head. "Just say what you have to say. I don't feel like playing games today."

He put his hands in his pockets. "I love Meri," he said to the bike. "I truly do and I always have. Even after we stopped speaking to each other, I still thought that if I waited long enough maybe someday she would change her mind about me. Even after . . ." He cut himself off. His head dipped and his shoulders slumped.

"If you really loved her you'd stop chasing her. You would let it go and leave her alone."

It was a dumb thing to say and I felt stupid after I said it, but I didn't like the thought of him flirting with Meri after I was gone. Not that I thought she'd do any flirting of her own. She'd be more likely to kill him than to kiss him. I just didn't like the idea of it.

"Yep. Let it go." He nodded slowly. I watched a wrinkle on the back of his neck crease and uncrease. "That's what all the books say to do. Always seemed like crazy advice to me, telling you to do the opposite of what you wanted to do most." He threw a glance at me from over his shoulder. "Is that what you're doing?"

"What?"

"Do you love her so much that you're letting it go?"

"What are you talking about?" I asked with a frown.

He turned around to face me again, his shoulders set in a tired slouch. "I've known Meri all my life. I've never seen her look the way she looks when she talks about you," he said. "Her whole face changes. Her eyes light up from the inside, and it's like I don't know who she is anymore." He smiled a twisted half smile that was both amused and bitter. "It's enough to make a grown man cry."

"When did she ever talk to you about me?"

"Right around noon today. She came by here after she talked to Auntie Bea and she didn't even have a gun or anything." He sighed a weary whoosh of air. "She loves you. You really ought to think about staying."

"But she told me to leave."

He shook his head. "If she did, it was just because she was scared. I'd be willing to bet that she didn't think you would. You're used to being the center of attention. You know what to expect and how to handle things. She's never been the center of any kind of scandal. It just scared her, that's all. I know she doesn't want you to leave."

"She told you who I am?" A flutter in my chest rose up to tickle the base of my throat.

He chuckled. "No, I already knew who you were. I recognized you that first time in the barn. I don't have much to do besides fix cars and watch TV. I've seen you on it a couple times, the *Power and Politics* show or something like that."

I'd been on that show dozens of times, always standing at my father's elbow, smiling and looking pretty. "Who did you tell?" I asked him softly and wondered, again, how far it was to the Arctic Circle. Maybe I could lose myself in tundra or hide out with the polar bears.

He tilted his head to one side. "I told Aunt Beatrice, but that's all. It's not anybody else's business."

"I don't understand what business it is of hers."

"Auntie's a huge fan of yours." He grinned. "She's always been fascinated by your father's career in a weirdly negative kind of way. She thinks he's the devil's own spawn, out to destroy the middle class and outlaw apple pie or some such thing. Ever since your big escape, she's been rooting for you to get away from him and find something for yourself in the world. Mind you, I don't think Meri is quite what she had in mind." His smile turned soft and wistful. "She's always loved politics. Crazy old woman.

Nuttier than a fruitcake."

"So why does she need to know that I'm here in Laurelvalley?"

He shrugged. "You know Meri went to see her this morning, right?"

"Right." I wasn't likely to forget.

"Well, of course, Aunt Beatrice was livid. I mean the kitchen floor thing was a pretty big shock to her." He held up his hands when he saw my jaw drop. "Auntie told me about that, not Meri."

I shut my mouth, but my cheeks grew uncomfortably warm.

"You have to understand what it meant to her. She was just stunned at first, but when she got around to thinking, it made her mad enough to spit nickels. Auntie's got her own ideas about how things should be." Taylor looked at his hands and pulled out his rag to rub at a spot of oil on his palm. "She was looking forward to Meri having a baby boy someday, sort of to replace her lost brother. You know, carry on the family genes and stuff. She never had the chance to marry, and so she holds on pretty fierce to the idea that life should be lived traditionally if you have the opportunity. Auntie threatened Meri with all kinds of dreadful things unless she got herself married soonest."

"I told her that's what would happen."

"And it did." Taylor tucked the rag back into his pocket and folded his arms across his chest. "How do you suppose Meri answered her?"

I didn't have to think very hard about that one. "I'm sure she told her aunt that, no matter what, she wouldn't marry you."

"True enough," he said, nodding his head. "That's pretty much what she said." He held up a finger and waved it at me. "But she also told her that she wouldn't marry anybody else either. Meri told Aunt Beatrice that she's in love with you and that she intends to build her life with you and henceforth, from this day forward, Auntie was to please phone before she came over."

"Oh." I remembered Meri's flickering headlights and her

94

waving arms. A glimmering of hope shivered through me. It weakened my knees, and I had to lean against the tool bench.

Taylor's eyes crinkled at the corners. "As you can imagine, Auntie nearly had a stroke," he said. "Disowned her right on the spot. Meri came over here right after and told me the whole story. Said she thought I should know why she had said no those four and some years ago and I was going to hear about it anyway, so I might as well hear it from her." Taylor's smile faded. "Makes a lot of sense to me now, but I sure wish she'd told me then. Maybe . . ." He seemed to shake himself away from the thought. "She hasn't forgiven me, but she says she's not looking to kill me anymore. I imagine I have you to thank for that."

I shrugged. He shrugged back.

"It's a start. Anyway, I went over to Auntie's and told her that I knew all about it and listened to her rant for a while. Then I told her who you were. It took her all of fifteen minutes to start planning to have you over for dinner some night soon." He shook his head and smiled. "Crazy old woman."

I wasn't smiling. My small glimmer of hope flickered and died. "She'll tell all her friends."

He nodded, still smiling. "Of course she will."

"They'll tell all their friends."

"People do like to talk," he agreed.

"My father will hear of it."

"Yep. That was sure to happen anyway. This is a very small town, you know. Secrets don't keep for very long."

I sagged against the bench. "I still have to leave."

"No," he said, his grin finally fading. "No, you don't. There's your mistake." He uncrossed his arms and stared at me hard. "Look, I still love Meri, and I expect I always will, but I respect her right to choose her own loves, and she's chosen you. Now, the way I see it, the only question left is, will you choose her?"

"No, that's not the question," I said emphatically. "That never was a question." I stood up straight and squared my shoulders. "The only question is when will my father come and how angry will he be when he gets here? I have to leave so Meri and this whole town won't suffer because of me."

"We won't." He turned and started lowering the bike lift, the air puffing out like a long, slow sigh.

"You don't understand my father."

"He's a man, right? So, sure I understand him."

"It's not as simple as that."

"True." He smiled. "Let me put it like this. Most people in the world, men and women, get this incredible urge at some point in their lives to collect something that they can pass on to the next generation. My father, when he died, left me his collection of old medicine bottles and faded cigar tins. He got the collection from his father and then passed it on to me like it was all the tea in China. Even I, my own self, have this odd itch to keep it safe so I can pass it on to my children, if I ever have any. Your father, now, he's collected himself an empire." He smiled at me and winked. "A man with an empire must have a mighty powerful itch."

"He does."

Taylor nodded. "That's good."

"How is that good?"

"It's good because we can use it." He unlocked the wheel clamp and rolled the bike off the lift. "I have a plan, and if it works, everybody will be happy in the end." He grinned at me wide enough to split his face. "And I do mean everybody."

I drove slowly back to the house with the trees throwing long shadows across the road. Sunlight flickered on and off in my eyes with wild confusion. My knees were trembling, and I could hardly feel my hands on the handlebars. Taylor's plan was a crazy one, but with the right timing and a little luck, it just might work. Everyone could be happy.

I could be happy.

The thought unnerved me and made me shake even more. I'd been happy staying with Meri, even with the threat of my father looming over us. I couldn't begin to imagine what that happiness would feel like when there was nothing hanging over our heads other than our own future. My knees shook so hard that I could hardly lift my foot to shift. I turned into the drive, tires crunching softly, the bike purring quietly beneath me.

Meri's truck was still in the same place I'd seen it last. The door was still open. Sergeant was pacing the fence, tossing his head and whinnying loudly. I drove off the gravel and around the truck. Meri lay curled in the middle of the drive, her hair spilling over the rocks, her skirt bunched around her thighs.

"Oh god," I whispered and jumped off the bike letting it fall. I ran up the drive and knelt beside her. She was shivering violently, her breath coming in gasps and sobs, hands balled into fists pressed tight against her eyes. Her knees were scraped and bloody.

"Meri?" I touched her cheek and smoothed the hair away from her face.

"Go away," she said, her voice high and tight.

"Are you hurt?" I asked. "Did you fall?"

"You didn't even . . ." She lifted her head. "You just . . ." Her mouth opened and closed around the words she couldn't form. "You left," she said, her voice cracking.

"Yes, but I came back."

"Why?" It was more than one question. It was a thousand questions, and each one had a thousand answers.

I brushed my hand through her hair, letting the soft glow of it slip between my fingers. I imagined it streaked with gray, her face lined, her hands knobby and frail, and it pleased me. I liked the thought of us growing old together. I liked the thought of belonging somewhere, to someone, especially if that someone was Meri.

"Why did you come back?" she asked again.

"I live here."

"You live here," she repeated, "with me?"

I looked up at the house with its red tinned gables, the gray barn and white board fences, the misty blue mountains peaking above the treetops dressed in a thousand shades of green. I looked down at her again. "This is my home. We're a family, you and me."

She reached for me, grabbed the collar of my jacket, and pulled me down to her. She cradled my head against her chest, burying her fingers deep in my hair, stroking and kneading. I lay with her on the gravel, my ear to her breast, and listened to the wild beating of her heart.

"What about your father?" she asked, her hands dropping suddenly.

I raised my head and grinned. "Taylor has a plan."

She lifted her hands and cradled my face in her palms, thumbs rubbing hard across my cheekbones. "I'll bet it's insane."

"Oh, it is. You're going to hate it." I leaned down and kissed her. She returned my kiss, open mouthed, pressing hard, her palms squeezing my face. Our lips came away warmed and wet.

"Upstairs?" she asked in a whisper.

I kissed the tip of her nose. "Anywhere you want." I licked my thumb and rubbed it over the worst of her mascara smudges. "Even right here, right now."

She laughed and hugged me to her. Sergeant gave a loud wet snort from his side of the pasture fence. We both looked up to see him cantering away, his tail held high and his neck strongly arched.

"I don't think he approves," Meri said. "He's worse than Aunt Beatrice." Her face fell. "I think I'm going to miss her."

"Don't start missing her just yet. We're supposed to have dinner with her next Tuesday."

Meri's eyes went wide. "We, as in both you and me? Together?"

"Well, to be honest, she just wanted me, but she doesn't mind if you tag along."

"Taylor?" she asked.

I smiled. "He can come too if you want." She scowled at me

and I sighed softly. "He fixed things for you as best he could, Meri."

"I don't think I like that idea."

"You've still got some time to get used to it." I sat up and pulled her with me. She winced a little for her knees. The blood on them had dried, but the scrapes still looked raw. "You think we need to go get your knees stitched?"

"Nah," she said with sparkle in her eye, "a couple of Band-Aids, they'll be just fine."

Chapter Five: PLANS

The first gusts of autumn blew down from the mountains, the chilly breezes ruffling through fading leaves, wilting the summer greens into dull yellows and reds. My chores became more pleasant now that the hot, sticky part was over and also more onerous because there were a lot more of them. There was always the usual mucking to do, Sergeant being so full of himself, and pastures to mow, hay to bale and bring in. But now there were fields to fertilize, earth to turn and what seemed like a thousand apples trees to pick, each with a million apples to sort and pack according to type. In spite of the early spring frost, or maybe because of it, it had been a good year for apples.

An odd assortment of Meri's cousins came over to help with the harvest. I got to help this time too, climbing one tree and then moving on to the next, baking apples in one color box, cider apples in another. The eating apples we kept for ourselves and for Sergeant, too. The broken ones we threw into a barrel for

Taylor's promise of apple wine. Meri refused, at first, to have anything to do with Taylor, plan or no plan, but the hint of the rewards proved to be greater than her hate. I knew it would. Meri's hatred was a reasonable one, and by the end of the summer, it had faded to an intense dislike. So we threw the broken apples into a barrel, laughed and sang, ate and drank, fought and made up. It was the best October I'd ever known and Meri just kept smiling in a bone-tired but satisfied kind of way.

Taylor had been right when he said that running a farm was almost impossible for one person to do alone. It was hard enough for two and some temporary cousin power. I don't know how Meri did it all and still found the time to run a B&B before I arrived. I thought it was too much, and to my surprise, Meri agreed. She took down the sign, wrapped it carefully in an old blanket and stored it in the tack room in the barn. Even so, it still seemed like there was always something else that needed doing. We were always sweating or stinking or covered in muck. My pale skin acquired a deepening tan and my arms the suggestion of biceps. Calluses blossomed across my palms.

I absolutely loved it.

Today, though, I was still lying in bed, sick to my stomach and excused from chores. I was glad of it too, because the day had dawned wet and cold. Rain pattered against the windowpanes while Meri puttered softly around the room. I huddled under the sheets, trying to get my mind off the queasiness that fluttered in my stomach by reciting multiplication tables in my head. I was working on the elevens when I got bored.

I peeked out from under the sheets. "Are my gills still green?" I asked Meri in a shaky voice.

She stopped in the middle of folding a freshly laundered T-shirt and looked me over with a critical eye. "That's 'green around the gills,' and the answer is yes. I'd say that you were still looking pretty pasty."

"And outside it's still raining hard?"

"Like a cow on a flat rock."

I already knew that it was because I could hear the rain pattering against the window. I just wanted to hear her say the one about the cow and the flat rock. It was a funny picture. "You think Sergeant will be all right?"

She smiled. "He generally has enough sense to come in out of the rain, but I'll go check on him in a little while."

She finished folding the T-shirt into a neat, precise square and put a short stack of them into the dresser drawer. I still didn't know how to do that. I was just at the point where I was beginning to believe her when she said that clothes didn't just disappear from the hamper, wash themselves and magically reappear in the dresser drawers every Friday afternoon. Meri kept telling me that there was no such a thing as the laundry fairy, but I was strongly resisting the idea. Still, I tried to help out as much as I knew how. My folded T-shirts always ended up asymmetrical and rhomboid-ish, but Meri was very patient and didn't seem to mind refolding when she thought I wasn't looking. She still wouldn't let me cook very often. That bothered me some, but I was getting used to meat and potatoes, and once in a rare while Meri broke down and bought something for me she considered exotic, like asparagus or an artichoke.

I swallowed hard and pulled the covers higher. This particular morning, even the thought of food made my stomach flip around in an uncomfortable way.

"Would you like some ginger ale?" she asked, pulling a pair of jeans from the hamper.

My stomach rose a little higher into my throat. "God, no."

She laughed softly and shook the jeans out. Three quick tucks, some magic sleight of hand, and she had another perfect square. "How about if I rub your feet? Do you want me to do that?"

I thought about it for a second. "No, I don't want you to do that either. It would give me too many conflicting feelings. I'd want to kiss you and throw up at the same time."

102

"Ew," she said with a little shiver. "You could've talked all day and not said anything like that."

That funny saying was a new one to me, and I was still puzzling it out when the phone rang. Meri set the jeans on top of a perfectly square pile of pants and went down to the kitchen to get it. I hadn't been able to talk her into getting a phone installed upstairs. She didn't understand why anybody would need more than one, and that one belonged in the kitchen. I couldn't even talk her into putting one in the barn. She claimed it would make me too lazy and if I had anything I needed to say to her I could just 'walk my skinny butt back to the house and say it,' I think is how she put it. My butt wasn't nearly as skinny as it was when I first arrived, but still, she was probably right. Meri came back upstairs and sat next to me on the side of the bed.

"Aunt Beatrice wants to come over," she said, leaning over me to tuck the sheet in around my shoulders. "I told her you were sick and not up to receiving visitors. She's coming anyway."

I groaned and Meri smiled. There wasn't much you could do with Aunt Beatrice once she got hold of an idea.

"I'll move to the parlor." I struggled to get out from under the sheets while fatigue and nausea conspired to keep me in them.

Meri laid a firm hand on my shoulder and pushed me into the pillow. "I told her you were in bed, so stay in bed."

"I'm in your bed, Meri. I don't think she's ready for that. She still won't sit with us at the kitchen table."

Meri grinned evilly. "She'll just have to get ready. After all those ridiculous dinners we've had to attend with her showing you off to the neighbors like a prize-winning rutabaga, she can stand stepping into our world for a little while."

I gave her a look and she gave me one back. She made a funny face at me and I crossed my eyes and stuck out my tongue.

"Promises, promises," she said pinching my cheek. "Maybe when you're feeling a little better." She bent over to kiss my scars and touch my cheek with hers. "You're still feeling a little clammy."

"Not very sexy, is it?"

She tried not to smile. "No, not really."

That wasn't the answer I was looking for, and it didn't do much to bolster my slowly unraveling self-image. I had changed so much since I first crash-landed in Meri's barn. Physically speaking, I didn't think it was all for the better. I looked at her. "Am I getting ugly?"

She touched my cheek. "No, Bea, of course you're not. You're beautiful even when your gills are green."

I felt my eyes tear and the room went wavy. "I don't like the way you say that."

"Oh, Bea," she said, laughing at me, her eyes going all sparkly.

"I am getting ugly," I said pulling the sheet over my head. "You're just too polite to admit it."

She kissed me through the sheet. The fabric made her mouth feel all scratchy and stiff. "You're so cute when you're emotional," she said. Her words warmed the cloth near my cheek.

"Well, I'm glad you like it," I snapped at her.

Her fingers traced the cloth around my chin making small shushing noises as they slid across the fabric. "You want that ginger ale now?" she asked.

I thought about drinking it, and my stomach held steady. "Yes, please."

With another kiss through the sheet, she got up and I heard her go down the stairs. Even with a steady stomach, I was still feeling really tired, and I hoped that Aunt Beatrice wasn't going to make me get out of bed. I stared into the sheets. They had little yellow flowers on them and I counted the petals, wondering what kind of flowers they were supposed to be. Probably something with a name that sounded like a disease, like clematis or nasturtium. A gust of wind rattled the rain against the widows, and I thought of all the fading flowers out in the garden. Meri and I had worked hard that summer, cleaning her mother's old kitchen plot, trimming the bushes, planting new flowers and even some herbs for the sake of tradition. Now the garden was beginning to get that brownish ragged edged look that happened after autumn's first frost. It had been such a beautiful summer. I was sorry to see it go.

Meri came back up the stairs. She lifted the corner of the sheet and peeked under it at me.

"Ginger ale's on the nightstand," she said. "I brought you a few crackers, too."

"Thank you," I said looking at her, studying her face. Today, her eyes were a clear pale blue. The pinched lines around them had long since disappeared, and there was a certain set to her mouth that made it look like she was always just on the verge of smiling. My heart swelled. I sniffed and then she did smile, shaking her head. She pulled the sheet down farther and kissed my lips softly. She pressed her cheek against mine.

"I love you too, Bea."

She did. No question about it. Sometimes that nearly scared me to death. I reached for her hand. "Do you really think Taylor's plan will work?"

She sat on the edge of the bed and stroked the back of my hand with her fingertips. "I think it just might."

"We're taking such a big chance."

"I know." Meri reached over and put a hand on my stomach. "All of us are."

I put my hands on top of hers. "I wish it was over."

"Yeah," she said with a slight sag to her shoulders. "Me too. I don't know what's taking so long. I thought for sure that the news of your being here in this little pond would have floated down to the ocean by now." She tilted her head and looked thoughtful. "We'll give it another week or two, and then we'll start jumping around and waving flags to get your father's attention."

"Why don't we just wait?" I asked, pressing her hand against my stomach. "Maybe he's forgotten all about me. Maybe he won't ever come."

Meri looked at our hands. "The whole plan is complicated

enough as it is. If we wait much longer, it'll be too hard on you and too much of a shock for him to be useful." Meri frowned, her brows creasing with concern.

"Are you having regrets, Meri?"

"No, Bea, no regrets. Just a few little fears, that's all. I want us to be a family. I just can't see what shape that family is going to take."

"Can anybody?"

"I guess not." Meri drummed her fingers over my bellybutton. "Maybe we should start jumping around waving flags right now."

"You mean you'll have Sam put my picture in the paper?"

"Yep," she said. A mischievous grin twitched at her lips. "I've been saving the one I took of you at the Fourth of July picnic."

"The pie eating one?" I asked. The question ended with a squeak.

"That's the one." She nodded happily. "It's a surefire bet that it'll attract attention."

I narrowed my eyes. "You wouldn't . . ."

"Why not?" She laughed. "It's such a funny picture. You had a cherry stuck up your nose. Wouldn't everyone in the whole world just love to see a picture of Collier Torrington with a cherry stuck up her nose? I bet we can get good money for it, too."

I rolled over with a moan and pulled the covers over my ears.

"God, how embarrassing," I said. "If you put that picture in the paper, I'll never get to be president." I moaned again as dramatically as I could. "There goes my whole career."

Meri chuckled at that. She knew that even though I was intimately familiar with the political machine, I was just about as ambitious as her prize-winning rutabaga. She leaned over me and rested her chin on my shoulder, her arm slipping around my middle. "We had such a wonderful time at the picnic. Everybody liked you, and no one even looked cross-eyed at us being together."

I hugged her arm against me. "It was the best picnic I've ever been to, but I think people were still too dazed to look cross-eyed. Give it time. Someone will get all worked up about it and then we'll be banished back to the farm." I snuggled deeper into her arms. "That's okay with me though. I like it here."

The doorbell rang.

"That must be the Auntie," Meri said sitting up. "I really love that she rings the doorbell now." She gave my butt a quick rub and went downstairs.

Aunt Beatrice wouldn't come upstairs.

The ginger ale and crackers settled my stomach a little so I dragged myself out of bed, threw on a robe and went down to the parlor. She was waiting for me, sitting with Meri on the couch and chatting about the apple harvest, falling prices and asking if the cousins had done a good job for her this year. She was in her Sunday clothes, a powder blue jacket and skirt with a small matching hat perched precisely on top of her blue helmet of hair. A small blue handbag sat at her feet.

She sipped daintily at a glass of iced tea, pinky finger raised slightly. I sat myself in the wingback chair and propped my feet on the ottoman. My hair was a mess and the robe was an old one. I was aware that I wasn't dressed properly for receiving visitors, but still, I didn't care very much for Auntie's slim, disapproving frown. I never failed to entertain her guests during one of her dinners, but this was my own home, and I'd be damned if I was going to try to meet expectations on a Saturday when I was tired and sick.

Auntie set her glass of tea on a coaster. She glanced at me again and then turned to Meri. "I phoned Taylor, too. He's on his way over."

Meri's polite smile turned instantly into a glare. "Aunt Beatrice, this is not a good time. Bea really isn't feeling very good."

"Yes, I can see that," she said with a little sniff and a quick cut of her eyes in my direction. She folded her hands in her lap. "It can't be helped. God works things out all in His own time. We can't always see to His purposes."

I set my feet back on the floor. When Aunt Beatrice invoked religion, it usually meant that she was distressed about something. The last time she mentioned God in casual conversation was when her trashcan caught on fire and she burned her garage to the ground.

"Auntie Bea," I said to her gently, "has something happened?"

Auntie reached down and picked up her purse. She held it in her lap, her hands clutching at it tightly. She suddenly looked small and frightened.

Meri leaned forward and touched her arm. "Auntie," she said, "if there's something you need us to help you with, all you have to do is ask." Meri raised an eyebrow. "You haven't been vacuuming out the fireplace again have you?"

Auntie pursed her lips and shook her head. Meri turned to look at me with both eyebrows raised. I shrugged slightly. Auntie fumbled with the clasp of her purse, opened it and pulled out one of her embroidered linen handkerchiefs. She dabbed at the corner of her eye.

"Harvey called me just a little while ago," she said to Meri and then turned to me. "He's our mayor. We're very close. He calls me for advice all the time."

I suppressed a smile, but it was hard. "Yes, Aunt Beatrice, I know. Meri's told me all about it."

Auntie sat up a little straighter and gave Meri a prim, pleased little smile. "Well, he got a call from Bobby Duncan. Bobby runs the airstrip out off Highway Two Fifty-two. Mostly for crop dusting, you know."

Both Meri and I nodded at her. Auntie opened her mouth, closed it again and pressed her handkerchief against her lips.

"What did Bobby say, Auntie?" Meri asked.

"Bobby told Harvey that three large men in dark suits and sunglasses arrived at the terminal just a little over an hour ago."

She lowered the hankie and leaned forward over her handbag. "Harvey said that Bobby said that they all had those little thingies in their ears and were standing around the building drinking black coffee and giving his flight control operator the third degree." She slumped against the couch and pressed the hankie to her mouth again. "What are we going to do?" she cried from behind the hankie. "I love this town, and I don't want to see it turned into a trash dump. I don't want a prison in my backyard."

I shot Meri a sharp look and she had the grace to blush. "That's not going to happen, Auntie. I promise you, I'll never let that happen."

"What are you going to do?" she asked her eyes bright and shining. She leaned forward toward me, clutching her purse tight against her. "You should run, Collier. You should go. You should go right now. Go pack your things. Hop on your motorcycle and zoom away from here."

I glanced at Meri who was looking amused. Aunt Beatrice was a woman of great passions, and I just happened to be one of them. Or, at least, she was passionate about the idea of me. The real me tended to disappoint her a little.

"I can't go, Auntie," I said to her gently. "There are things that hold me here."

Auntie shot Meri a hateful look and then turned to me again. She spoke slowly and distinctly as if I could understand her better that way. "Collier, your father is coming."

I couldn't help smiling. Over the past few months I had listened, ad nauseam, to Aunt Beatrice tell me how evil my father was and how he epitomized everything that was wrong with America today. It was the idea of him that she hated. I had a feeling that when she met him, he would disappoint her a little bit, too.

"We have a plan, Auntie, that we think will work, but I want you to know that if it comes down to it, I won't put this town in jeopardy. If I have to leave, I will," I promised, mostly for the sake of her comfort, which tended to have a direct impact on mine.

She sniffed and dabbed again at her eyes leaving a little dot of lipstick high on her cheek. "You're just the sweetest girl, Collier. I told that man, that in spite of everything, you were a credit to us all."

"What man?" Meri asked.

"The man at the post office, dear." She turned her head toward me. "He said that he already heard you were here, Collier, and was asking after you. He was a very nice polite young man, if a little on the thin side. I told him he needed to eat more. I offered to bake him a pie." She turned back to Meri. "Surely I told you about all that."

I sat very still. Meri slouched in her seat and drummed her fingers on the arm of the couch.

"No, Auntie," she said. "You must have forgotten."

"Well," Auntie said with a flip of her hankie, "it was about a week ago, right before the ladies auxiliary meeting. It was my turn to host. I'm sure you remember," she said knowing that we couldn't have forgotten yet since our attendance had been required even over our strong objections. "I was so busy I must have forgotten to mention it."

"What exactly did you talk to him about, Auntie?" I asked. Even to me, my voice sounded thin and strained. Meri looked over at me and her eyes widened a little. I must have gone pale. I certainly felt pale.

"We talked about you, Collier, of course. I told him that you, who everyone around here calls 'Bea' for some silly reason, were living with my niece. I said that you were a very great help with the farm work, that you plowed a straight row and had a very good hand for ornery old horses. I told him that you seemed to be very happy, not that I approved or anything, you understand, but one needs to let people find their own way."

"Did he understand what it was that you didn't approve of?" I asked, shooting a quick, frightened glance at Meri.

Aunt Beatrice pressed her hankie against her chest. "I did have to be blunter than I would have liked to have been." She shook her head sadly. "I said that I didn't approve of your sort of life-style, and he asked what was wrong with farming. I told him he was being silly. Nothing was wrong with farming. I used to farm, my parents farmed, everyone around here farms to some degree. It's a good, wholesome life. But two women living together like a married couple, well that's just unnatural." She gave a little start as if she suddenly remembered it was the unnaturals that she was speaking to. "I'm sorry, my dears. I don't mean to be so direct. I love you both, but I just can't approve of it."

I took a deep breath, closed my eyes and let it out slowly. I considered counting to ten, but I didn't think that worked for fear. "Auntie, was the man really, really thin, with short red hair, wire glasses and squinty eyes?"

Auntie appeared surprised. "Yes, I believe so."

My heart dropped into my toes. I looked at Meri. "That must have been Wesley, my father's personal secretary. Everyone calls him Weasel. Anything he knows, my father knows."

"Shit," Meri said dropping her head into her hands.

"Meri Margaret Donovan!" Auntie said, pressing her hankie harder against her chest. "You will not use that language in my presence."

"Sorry, Auntie Bea," Meri said automatically. She lifted her head. Her face was pinched and pained. "That changes everything."

I nodded, not trusting myself to speak. My father hadn't even arrived and the plan was already in shambles.

"He won't believe that you're married to Taylor," Meri said to me.

I shook my head.

Auntie's eyes lit up. "Collier, when did you marry Taylor? Why didn't you tell me? Why wasn't I invited?"

I shook my head. "I didn't marry Taylor, Auntie, that's just what we were going to tell my father." I held my hands over the fluttering in my stomach. "We thought that if he thought I was already married, he would go away and leave us alone."

"Oh, sweet Jesus, bless us and save us. What a ridiculous notion," Auntie spluttered, looking indignant. "That wouldn't be enough."

"Yes, Auntie," Meri said, "we know that. That's why we went a little further with it, sort of for insurance."

"Gracious Lord, have mercy, and all the saints preserve us," Auntie said, fluttering her hankie underneath her chin. "What have you girls done?"

Meri made a funny sound, a choked laugh that was more than half a sob. "We thought it would be more convincing if Bea was to have Taylor's baby."

"Excuse me?" Auntie's voice dropped low.

"Bea is pregnant with Taylor's baby," Meri said in precisely clipped words.

"Right now?" Aunt Beatrice asked.

"Yes," I answered and my stomach made a funny gurgling sound. "For about three months now. We thought it would add some weight to our argument." I looked down at my ankles that seemed slightly swollen to me, even if Meri swore it was too early for that.

Auntie stood abruptly, her purse falling to the floor. She glared at Meri and then at me, her eyes snapping angrily. "How did this happen?" she asked and then shook her head. "No, no, don't tell me how. I don't want to know. Just tell me what you thought such an ungodly thing as bearing a child out of wedlock would accomplish." She set her hands to her hips. "And why didn't you tell me about all this?"

"We didn't want you to worry, Auntie," Meri said. "Taylor was going to tell you right after we talked to Bea's father."

"You should have talked to me before," she said with a petulant pout and a worried crease of her brow. "What in God's name were you two thinking?"

"Auntie," I said, "my father wants a grandchild more than anything in the world. We were going to offer him a chance to have one, on the condition that he leaves us alone." I rubbed at my stomach and the slight pooch rounding the front of my pajamas. It wasn't the baby showing yet, just Meri's potatoes. "That is, we intended him to think that he was leaving me and Taylor alone, which he might have agreed to. But if he knows about Meri and me, he won't leave us alone, no matter what."

Auntie sank onto the couch. "Whose silly idea was this?" she asked.

"Taylor's," Meri said, rubbing at her temples. "He thought that it would make everybody happy. Bea's father would get a grandchild for his legacy, Taylor would get to be a part of our lives, you would get the niece or nephew you've always wanted, and Bea and I could live our lives together." She looked over at me miserably. "It might have worked."

"It would not have worked," Auntie said sharply. "Lies never work, Meri. You were raised with better sense than that."

Meri nodded her head slowly and it sank into her hands. "I'm sorry, Auntie," she said. "It's just that I love Bea so much. I would agree to anything that would give us a chance at being a family."

Auntie Bea pressed her hankie to her lips. She looked stricken. My skin prickled into goose bumps, and I shivered at the sudden chill. The butterflies rose from my stomach and began swirling around in my throat.

I think the plan might have worked, at least for a time, but my father wouldn't care how much Meri loved me. He wouldn't care how empty either of our lives had been before we found each other. He would just be very, very angry. He would understand that his suspicions about me had been true, and Meri would become a problem that he had to solve by whatever means necessary. I shivered again as my stomach twisted into knots and rose to touch the back of my tongue. I jumped up, both hands covering my mouth, and rushed down the hallway to the bathroom.

• • •

Meri sat on the floor beside me, rubbing her hand in small circles across my back. I was still kneeling with my cheek pressed

113

against the porcelain rim of the commode, a cold sweat still coating my skin. I had nothing left to throw up, but every time I thought of my father and what he might do to Meri, I found myself racked with dry heaves. I started shivering. Meri reached, pulled a towel off the towel rack and draped it across my shoulders. I lifted my head and leaned against her. She held my head to her shoulder, her cheek pressed to my forehead. She felt so warm and safe, it made me want to cry, but my body had nothing left in it.

I heard footsteps just outside the door and raised my eyes. Taylor's head popped around the corner.

"Ladies," he said with a tip of his ball cap. He focused on me and frowned. "Jesus, Bea, you look like death warmed over."

"She's sick, Taylor," Meri said sharply.

"I can see that," he answered. "You need me to run to the store or something? Get you some chicken noodle soup or maybe some ice cream or pickles?"

"Oh, god," I said, pushing away from Meri and leaning over the commode. My body heaved and spasmed. There was still nothing left, but my stomach kept pretending.

"Shut up, Taylor," Meri said, holding on to my shoulders.

"Hey, I'm sorry," he said. "I was just trying to help."

"Why don't you try being helpful, then?"

"Like how? You're already patting her back, and she doesn't have any hair to hold. So what am I supposed to do?"

"Be useful, for a change. Why don't you go plow the back forty or something?"

"It's October."

"Oh, for god's sake, Taylor, just go away," Meri nearly shouted.

"Easy there, babe," I heard him say. "Don't get your knickers all in knot. Auntie asked me to drop everything and come over, and so I'm over. Suppose you tell me why I'm here if you don't want me to be."

Meri's grip on my shoulders tightened and then relaxed. She

114

rubbed at them briskly and that settled me enough so I could lean against her again. She wrapped her arms tight around me.

"I'm sorry, Taylor," she said, failing to sound like she really meant it. "I'm just a little jumpy." I felt her chest rise and fall. "I don't know why Auntie called you to come over. Maybe she wanted you for moral support or something."

"Why?" he asked. "What'd she burn this time? I mean, besides the phone lines."

"Nothing. If you want to know exactly what she wanted, you'll have to wait and ask her."

"Yeah, okay," he said. "Where is she?"

Meri put her hand on my head and started stoking my hair. "She ran out to get Bea some Pepto-Bismol. I told her we weren't having a problem with that end, but you know Auntie Bea. It's her cure-all for anything that ails you."

"Right, I remember," he said with grimace. "So what's going on here then? I know why Bea's sick, but why are you so jumpy?"

"My father's coming," I whispered.

Taylor lifted his cap and scratched underneath. He settled it on his head again with a little yank on the brim. "Isn't that a good thing? We did plan on that, you know."

"It would've been a good thing," Meri said, "if Bea's father didn't already know that she and I were living together in an intimate fashion."

"Oh." He crossed his arms and leaned against the doorjamb. "That's not such a good thing."

"No," I said, my voice sounding raw and raspy, "it's not a good thing at all."

"How did that happen?"

I felt Meri shift slightly. "Auntie was talking to strangers at the post office."

Taylor squeezed his eyes shut and leaned his head against the door jam. "We should have anticipated that."

"Well, we didn't," Meri said crossly.

"He's not going to believe that we're married," he said to me.

"No," I answered, "he's not."

"We really could get married."

"No!" Meri shouted and it made me jump. "That's not an option."

Taylor straightened, rubbed his face and stepped into the bathroom. I felt the tension creep into Meri, stiffening her back, tensing her shoulders. He squatted in front of us and peered at me closely. Meri's arms tightened into almost a squeeze. I couldn't see her face, but I know she must have been scowling pretty ferociously.

Taylor looked at her and tugged on the bill of his cap. "Meri, my darlin', you really need to calm yourself down. You're wound tighter than a cat at a dog show."

"I am not," she said through clenched teeth. I could feel the tremor in her arms, and I wondered if Taylor could see it.

Taylor reached out as if to feel my forehead, but Meri slapped his hand away.

"Don't touch her," she said harshly.

"Why not?" he asked. "You think she's contagious?"

Meri snorted. "You'd better hope not."

Taylor reached out again and Meri slapped at him again.

"Stop it. Just leave her alone. She's already sick enough because of you."

Taylor scratched at his beard stubble and sat on the bathroom floor. "Meri, Bea here, is carrying my child," he said, and Meri's arms squeezed even tighter around me. "I am naturally concerned about her and about the baby. I'm sorry that it disturbs you, but I would like to remind you that this is something we all agreed to do."

"I know." Meri's voice was barely a whisper, but it was heavy and full of regret.

Taylor opened his mouth to say something else, but I held up a hand and stopped him.

"Taylor, I don't think you understand what she's afraid of."

"No, I surely don't," he said with a sad shake of his head.
"Meri, let go of me."

She stiffened.

"Please," I said softly, "I want to look at you." Her arms slid open reluctantly. I sat up and turned to face her. "You're scaring yourself for no good reason, Meri."

"I don't want him touching you," she said, looking at her lap.

"He never has touched me. You went to the clinic with us every time, remember? Taylor was in one room and I was in another. You were at my side, holding my hand the whole time we were there, even during the really gross parts."

"I know."

"What you're afraid of just isn't going to happen."

"I know," she said again. "I know it in my head, but when he gets close to you, my heart goes all funny. You have a connection with him that I can't be a part of, and it scares me."

I took hold of her hand. "Meri, this is our child, yours and mine. Taylor's just the donor. My connection with him isn't any stronger than your connection with him through your shared past. I'm not going to fall in love with him, Meri, no more than you ever did," I said, reaching out to touch her cheek. "I can't. I'm already in love with you, and you fill my heart so completely that there isn't room for anyone else."

"Well, that's a fine how do you do," Taylor muttered under his breath.

Meri ignored him. "What about when the baby comes? Will I still be the only one in your heart then?"

"That's a different kind of love, Meri. It's one that you and I will share and grow into together." That sounded good, but I wasn't sure I believed it. It was the way it should be if ours was a perfect world, but I knew that life didn't always care about being fair. Still, I thought it was something Meri needed to hear, so I didn't feel bad about saying it.

Meri put her hand over mine and pressed her cheek hard against my palm. "I'm scared, Bea," she said almost in a whisper.

"I'm scared that something will take you away from me. I don't ever want to lose you again."

I leaned into her and touched my head to hers. "I don't know what's coming around the corner, Meri. I can't make you any grand promises, but I need you to trust me to do the right thing."

"I'm trying," she said, pressing harder against my hand.

Taylor cleared his throat. "You two aren't going to kiss, are you? Because, while I admit that the thought has its attractions, I'm not sure I'm prepared to see it happen."

Meri gave a sad little snort. "Taylor, you're such an asshole."

"That I will freely admit to, Meri, my love. But this asshole is still the father of that baby, and I am concerned about the ailing mother's dainty little ass being in prolonged contact with the cold tile."

I turned my head and looked at Taylor. "Could you say that again in English, please?"

"I think you should get the hell off the floor," he said. "How long do we have anyway to invent a plan B, or maybe we should call it plan C just so we don't get all confused. There's already too many Beas around here as it is."

Meri raised her head from mine and sat back, thinking. "I don't really know how long we have. Auntie said that Harvey heard from Bobby just about an hour ago, or more like two, I guess it would be now. If Bea's father is coming in from Washington, that's only an hour or so from here by air, and it takes an hour and a half to get here from the landing strip."

"Alrighty then, let's drop ten and punt." Taylor reached up and settled his cap firmly on his head. "Let's assume Bea's father will get here any minute." He jabbed a finger at me. "That means you need to get dressed. It'll be hard to argue your case while you're in a bathrobe."

"What case?" I asked him bitterly.

"We'll figure that out in a minute." He pointed at Meri. "And you, dear heart, you need to go take a swig of something strong.

Bea's going to need you at your calmest, nonviolent, level-headed best because shooting people is not an option here." Meri tensed and shot him an icy glare. Her arm twitched, and for a second, I thought she was going to hit him. He gave her a look that I couldn't fathom, but Meri suddenly flushed a bright red. Taylor looked a little surprised and then smiled just a bit. He looked down at himself and rubbed at his chest. "As for me, I need a change and a shave. Of course, the question remains, exactly what are we going to tell this father of yours?"

I stood slowly. My knees were a little shaky, but my stomach seemed to have finally worn itself out. I looked at Meri and Taylor, still sitting on the cold tile floor. "I think we should try something really daring."

"What's that?" Meri asked.

"I think we should just tell him the truth. Meet him head-on, so to speak. It won't work, but I can't think of anything else that's worth doing."

Taylor nodded his head slowly. "A novel approach. Bold and daring, yet subtle and clever. I like it."

Meri stood and slipped an arm around my waist. "Taylor, you really are an ass."

"Duly noted, Meri, my girl." Taylor touched the brim of his cap as he grinned up at us.

I brushed my teeth twice and got into the shower. The hot spray pummeled against my skin. All the clammy nauseousness that I had been feeling seemed to slough off me and circle around the drain. In spite of everything, I almost felt normal again. All our decisions were made. The hand had been dealt, and the only thing left was to wait and see how the cards would fall. I closed my eyes and tilted my head into the water, letting it wash over me.

The door opened and closed again, bringing with it a puff of cold air. I peeked out from behind the curtain. Meri stared at me for a long moment, her expression unfathomable, then she pulled her shirt over her head and dropped it on the floor. She stepped out of her shoes and unbuttoned her jeans, slid them down her legs and kicked them off. She pulled back the curtain and stepped into the shower, still wearing her socks and her underthings. I shifted a little to the side and let her step into the spray. She was shivering harder than if she were standing naked in a winter rain. The water dampened her hair and flattened it against her head. Rivulets ran down her face, bright drops hung on her eyelashes and on the tip of her nose. She slid her arms around my shoulders and pressed herself hard against me. I put my arms around her waist and held her until the water ran cold.

I stood in the parlor looking out the front window with a corner of the long gauzy curtains drawn back. Meri was sitting in the wingback chair, pale and pinched but no longer trembling. Taylor stood beside the fireplace, changed and shaven. I could hear their soft rustlings behind me, the shushing of Meri's jeans against the chair, the scuffing of Taylor's boots on the carpet, but I didn't turn around. I kept my eyes on the window. It had stopped raining, but the clouds still hung low in the sky, moving with a ponderous slowness, just barely brushing over the mountaintops.

The wind blew a strong gust and the trees bent and swayed as wet leaves tumbled across the yard. A long black limo turned into the drive. It moved with slow solemnity over the gravel. Three dark town cars trailed behind it like little goslings paddling after a mama goose. The curtains twitched in my hands. Seven months ago, I wouldn't have made that analogy. I glanced down at myself, at the clothes I had chosen, the shoes I had on, the tan of my hands, the pooch of my belly. The taste of Pepto-Bismol still coated my tongue. I was a real cousin now, and for that, I could forgive Aunt Beatrice for running off.

"He's here," I said without turning around.

The limo rolled to a stop, its long, sleek elegance sitting like a note of discord against the harmony of gravel and grass, blue mountains and wet blowing leaves. I watched Weasel jump out of the front and run around the limo to open the passenger door. My father unfolded his large frame from the car and stood for a moment studying the surroundings. I could see his hard eyes calculating the worth of the white clapboard house with its red tin roof, white board fences and the old rusty trucks. I blushed to think of how paltry it would seem tallied against his balance sheets. I wondered if some small part of him could see the beauty of it, or if he was too jaded by gilded edgings and swirled marble to understand what it was that surrounded him now. His expression gave nothing away, but it rarely did. His entourage of butt kissers and bodyguards closed in around him, and they moved as one toward the front porch.

I let the curtain fall. Meri stood as I walked over to her. I gave her hand a squeeze and her lips a quick brush with my own. There was a knock at the door and we all jumped. I squeezed Meri's hand again and went alone into the foyer to answer it.

When I opened the door, I stared up at two bodyguards I didn't recognize, large muscled men with crew cuts and dark suits, deep eyes and cleft chins. They were Secret Service types, not the usual goons for hire. I showed them my empty hands and they shifted to one side. My father stared down at me. He looked the same as he always did in his immaculate Armani suit, like the consummate politician with his neat steel gray hair, wise old face, cold piercing eyes. The eyes raked over my short hair, red flannel shirt and faded blue jeans. They returned to the scar on my forehead and lingered there. A slight tightening of his jaw was the only sign of his displeasure.

"Collier," he stated simply in his deep, rumbling voice. It was the sound of distant thunder. The warning before the storm.

"Daddy," I returned in my "being polite to strangers" tone of voice. "Won't you come in?"

His eyes narrowed a fraction. He looked at Weasel and jerked his chin. Weasel muttered instructions to the bodyguards. They shifted their positions, and my father stepped into the house with Weasel and only one guard behind him. It was a way of telling me that he didn't see this situation as much of a challenge or a threat and that he was in firm control of all things. I thought it a wasted gesture. I let him see that by turning my back to him as I led him into the parlor where Meri and Taylor stood waiting.

"Daddy, this is Meri Donovan and the gentleman is Taylor McNally."

He nodded minutely but didn't hold out his hand. I hadn't expected him to.

"Meri, Taylor," I continued. "This is my father, Senator Alfred Torrington."

Neither one of them even nodded. They stood silent and watchful. I went to stand in between them. We were all wearing flannel shirts, blue jeans and boots. The shirts had belonged to Meri's father. It was my own gesture, something that would have a deep significance for us and, at the same time, carry a message that I knew my father would understand immediately.

He did and he didn't like it. He sat down in the wingback chair and crossed his legs, set his elbows on the armrest and steepled his hands together. Weasel and the guard, a big man with baby blue eyes and a professional grade of blank face, positioned themselves on either side. Weasel stood behind the chair with one hand resting on the back. The guard stood a little to one side where nothing would interfere with his line of fire, but I didn't think it would come to that since Meri promised to keep her temper.

My father settled into the chair, owning it, possessing it, declaring his authority over everything in the room. "Get yourself packed, Collier," he said quietly. It was his "no options, no argument, dreadful consequences if you don't jump" tone of voice. "I'll give you ten minutes."

The voice stabbed straight into me. Conditioned as I was to obey it, I turned slightly and almost took a step forward, but

Meri put a hand on my shoulder. She squeezed lightly. Taylor put his hand on my other one.

I took a breath to steady myself and looked at my father in as direct a manner as I ever had. "No, Daddy."

His eyes narrowed a fraction more. Weasel frowned and shifted uncomfortably.

"I'm not asking," he said sharply.

"I'm not going," I shot back.

He looked almost confused. He could understand conniving and manipulating, begging and pleading. He expected such things from me, but a flat refusal was something new. His eyes hardened. They shifted to Taylor and then to Meri. "You don't belong here, Collier. Your place is with a different kind of people."

"I don't think so," I said leaning hard against Meri's and Taylor's hands. "My place is where I choose to make it. I choose here."

My father unsteepled his hands and sat up straight. He set his feet flat on the floor and grasped the armrests in his hands. It was his Pharaoh pose. He was about to issue an ultimatum.

"I'm not going to argue with you, girl. You've already wasted enough of my time. The senate is in session. There's a vote coming up, and I've lost a whole day over this. Go get packed right now, or I'm going to drag you out of here with just those rags that you're wearing."

Meri's hand tightened on my shoulder. The guard's eyes cut toward her, and he turned his body a fraction of a degree. I could tell by the set of his shoulders that, in spite of Taylor's muscles, he had pegged Meri as the biggest threat in the room if it came to using force. He was right. I raised my shoulder under Meri's hand just a bit, telling her to ease down. If she started anything, she would be the one most likely to get hurt. Her grip tightened. I wasn't sure if she was misunderstanding, not listening or telling me no. My guess was that she was telling me no. Force and violence weren't my father's preferred style. It didn't look good in the papers, and if he had left his goons behind that meant he

123

was concerned about looking good in the papers. But Meri didn't know he was bluffing, and I had no way of telling how short a fuse she was sitting on. There were more of them than there were of us. If she started it, we would lose.

I turned my attention back to my father. I decided to call the bluff, if only for Meri's sake. "Dragging me out of here wouldn't be a good idea, Daddy."

His eyebrows raised an almost imperceptible amount. "Why is that?"

"Because I won't go peacefully, and if you get your boys to drag me out of here kicking and screaming, you might hurt the baby." I played the only real card we had and hoped, after all we'd been through to get it, that it was worth something.

"The baby," he said flatly.

"I'm pregnant, Daddy. Taylor here is the father."

He glanced over his shoulder at Weasel who flicked his eyes over toward Meri and nodded his head. My father turned back to me. "Rumor has it that you're . . ." and he waved a hand in Meri's direction.

"I am."

"But you're carrying his child." He pointed his chin toward Taylor.

"Yes, Daddy."

"Collier," he said with some degree of exasperation, crossing his legs and steepling his hands again. "What have you gotten yourself into this time? You're making quite a mess of things here."

"I'm not making a mess," I said. "I'm making a life for myself."

My father started tapping his forefingers together. "You've angered your fiancé, you're sleeping with some woman, you're carrying a strange man's child, and you think that's not a mess? Do you have any idea how hard this is going to be for me to clean up?"

I swallowed hard and focused on the weight of Meri's and

Taylor's hands. "There's nothing here for you to clean up. Who I sleep with is nobody's business but mine, and the baby is still your grandchild, regardless of its paternity." I put my hands on my stomach. "If you want to be a part of this child's life, you will leave me alone to live with whom and how I please. We won't make trouble for you, Daddy. We just want to be left alone."

My father smiled a little half smile. It was part of an expression that he thought made him look benevolent and wise, but the smile usually meant that he had something truly nasty up his sleeve and was about to lay it down. It made me start to feel nauseous again.

"I'm concerned for you, Collier," he said, jutting his chin out a little farther. "You're obviously recovering from a serious head injury." His eyes locked on the scar on my forehead. "And you don't sound like yourself. I think the strain of being made pregnant by a strange man might be too much for you, especially if the pregnancy was forced on you." His eyes cut over to Taylor. I felt Taylor jerk and his hand slipped off my shoulder. "Maybe you need a short rest, someplace nice and quiet where you can recover from this terrible thing that's happened to you."

Weasel made agreeing noises from behind the chair. The guard took a half step forward, standing on the balls of his feet, as Meri stepped closer to me. My father sat there in his wingback chair looking truly concerned for my welfare, but there was a hint of satisfaction in the jut of his chin that he just couldn't hide. I closed my eyes to shut out the sight of him. He could do it. It just needed a doctor with a well-greased palm, a forged signature or two, some witnesses to say what he told them to say and two of his dead-eyed goons to drag me away. He had done it to my mother on more than one occasion, so that his "quiet place to rest," places neither quiet nor restful, became one of her greatest fears.

But I was not my mother. I opened my eyes again. "If you try to have me committed, Daddy, I can guarantee that you'll never see me or your grandchild again, not even if I have to live in a cardboard box under a bridge to hide from you."

Weasel looked almost shocked. He blinked at me and then bent to whisper something into my father's ear in a low, sibilant tone.

My father's chin rose. "You do understand, Collier, that this is a very conservative state you've removed yourself to," he said, squinting his eyes in a way that meant he was thinking hard, making new plans on the fly. "In most conservative states, being a . . . an avowed . . . living openly as a . . ."

"Lesbian," Weasel supplied the word for him with a leer and a smug smile.

"Yes, being one of those is grounds for being declared an unfit mother."

I looked over my shoulder at Meri, my eyes questioning. She shook her head and shrugged. I turned back in time to see a flash of triumph cross my father's face.

"Here are your choices," he said to me. "You can come home with me now, and we'll discuss plans for your future on the way, or you can go somewhere for a long rest, and your mother and I will provide your child with a nice normal home as soon as it's born."

Meri stepped in front of me. The guard took half a step closer, his knees loose, arms at the ready. She ignored him and glared at my father, standing stiffly with her hands balled into tight fists. "You just try it, mister, and you'll have one hell of fight on your hands." Her voice was low and menacing.

My father didn't even look at her. She meant nothing to him. He stood. Taylor stepped in front of both Meri and me. The guard stepped forward and put his hand on Taylor's chest, fingers steepled, ready to jab.

"I'd like to avoid any unpleasantness if we can, Collier," my father said to me.

"We're not going to just let you drag Bea out of here," Taylor said, "not without a fight. You're forgetting that the baby's mine, too, and I'm not about to give you custody of him, not for love nor money."

My father ran a hand across the lapel of his jacket, smoothing it down. "Mr. McNally, I don't know how you managed to gain influence over my daughter, but I'm sure it was by some illicit means. I wouldn't be surprised to learn that you are a man with a violent past." He shot a glance at Weasel who nodded his head vigorously. "I, on the other hand, am a respected public servant and kind and loving father." Meri's arm twitched. I grabbed it and pinned it against her side. "There is no court in this world that would deny me custody of my grandchild when given the choice between me and you."

Taylor's shoulders sank. He turned to look at me, eyes panicked. I shook my head just a little. It was also a bluff. A good one, but it was still just a trick. Taylor turned back around and drew himself up. "Well, I guess we'll just have to see about that. But for right now, you're not taking Bea anywhere."

I watched the guard reassess Taylor, dismiss him again and turn his attention back to Meri. Tension trembled down her arm. I couldn't see her face from where she was standing, but I was betting it was just as scary as his.

"Enough of this," my father snapped at me. "Come along, Collier. Now."

"No, Daddy."

He looked pointedly at the guard, who answered his look with a noncommittal tick of his head. He would do it if my father gave the order, but it would be messy. People would get hurt, which meant it might not spin well on the evening news.

"I see," my father said tugging on the sleeve of his jacket. He turned and nodded to Weasel. Weasel grinned. It was an ugly thing to see. "You have twenty-four hours to change your mind, Collier. I believe you understand the consequences."

He turned his back to us and walked out of the room. Weasel turned, throwing a smirk over his shoulder that promised very bad things, and followed on his heels. Weasel lived for consequences. The bodyguard backed out of the parlor, never taking his eyes off Meri until he had cleared the door. He stopped in the foyer, gave her a slight bow and disappeared. None of us moved a muscle until the front door quietly snicked shut.

Meri turned and wrapped her arms around my waist. I leaned into her and pressed my cheek against hers.

"Twenty-four hours and then what?" Taylor asked, rubbing at his chest.

I stared at the parlor door. "Twenty-four hours and then he gets nasty."

"That wasn't nasty?"

I shook my head slowly from side to side, my face rubbing against Meri's. "He's not even warmed up yet."

"Sheeit," Taylor said, reaching for the brim of the ball cap that wasn't there.

Meri and I made love with quiet, intense desperation. She kissed me deeply, her mouth eating at my lips, her whole body grinding against mine as if she were trying to break through my skin and crawl inside me. Her jagged breathing, the hard chafing of her hands and the soft sound of her *ohs* built and burned and spilled me over the edge. My body spasmed underneath her, my cries lost inside the heat of her mouth.

She was still tense and quivering. I turned her over and began a slow exploration, touching every part of her, trying to memorize every inch of her skin, every freckle, every hair, every bump, both outside and in, with my hands, lips and tongue. I kissed the arch of her brow, sucked at the swell of her breast, caressed her calves and licked long, wet lines over the backs of her knees. I slipped inside her and stroked the secret places that made her writhe and groan, while my tongue made slow, rhythmic circles over the swollen heat of her. She came with a sharp arch of her back and a muffled scream. Then she clutched at me and wept.

I held her tight as her body shook underneath me, her face wet against my neck, her hands pressing me hard.

"Don't go, Bea. Oh, god, please don't go."

"Hush, Meri," I said, stroking her hair. "Who said anything about going?"

"You don't have to say it," she said into my shoulder. "I can feel it all over you."

"What would you rather I do?" I asked her softly.

"Stay." Her arms locked around me nearly squeezing the breath out of my lungs. "Stay here with me and let whatever's going to happen just happen. We'll think of something."

I buried my face against her skin and inhaled the scent of her. She smelled like soap and saltwater, rust and copper pennies. "What can you think of in twelve hours that will grow my father a heart?"

"I don't know," she said, her arms loosening and falling to the side. Her hands rested lightly on my hips. "Something. There has to be something."

I raised my head. "You believe in miracles?"

Her eyes glittered. "I believe in you."

I touched my forehead to hers. "I'll come back, Meri. As soon as he's gone, I'll come right back."

She closed her eyes and shook her head so that it chafed against mine. "No, you won't. You won't come back here. You'll stay away to protect me and the town. I'll never see you again. I'll never get to see our baby."

I rolled to one side, pulled her to me and held her. There wasn't anything I could say to comfort her, no lie I could tell that she wouldn't see through. I had to run, and she knew that if I did, I would have to keep running. I couldn't come back here because this place would be watched. She would never see the baby. There couldn't be a baby now. The thought made me sad and angry at the wastefulness of it, but what choice was there? If I tried to stay here, my father would do terrible things to Meri, to this town and its people. If I went with him, he would still do terrible things to them, just for having inconvenienced him, and I promised Auntie that I wouldn't let that happen. The only thing left to do was to run and keep his attention focused on me. Running seemed like the best choice for everyone, even if Meri couldn't see it.

I stroked her hair and counted her breaths until she fell into a fitful sleep. I rolled quietly away from her, got up and went into the bathroom. I cleaned myself a little with a swipe of the washcloth here and there, dressed in blue jeans and an old sweatshirt that I dug out of the hamper. There was no point in going for the leathers. They didn't fit at all anymore. Meri was still asleep when I came out, her arm thrown over her eyes, her hair in disarray, the blond of it scattered all over the pillow. It glittered softly in the moonlight, a soft golden glow, pale yellow against the white pillowcase. She stirred with the soft sigh of a dream. I turned and slipped out of the room.

In my old room, I walked carefully, hopping lightly over the squeaky spots in the floorboards, the first and third. My saddlebags were in the cedar chest, still packed. I dug them out and tossed them over my shoulder. The stairs were dark, and every step creaked just a little. I stepped lightly trying not to wake Taylor who was sleeping on the sofa in the parlor, the shotgun near at hand. Just in case, he said. He needn't have bothered, but I didn't feel like arguing with him.

It was too dark to see the pictures in the stairwell, but I brushed each one of them lightly with the tips of my fingers as I passed them on the way down. The last frame, the picture of Sergeant and me, I knocked askew. I meant it as a message to Meri, a parting gesture, but I didn't know if she would hear what I was saying or not. Maybe it didn't even matter.

The kitchen door shut quietly behind me. I stood on the stoop and looked around the yard at the familiar things that seemed so strange in the gray monochrome of well after midnight, still far from morning. The air was chilly but not cold. The moon was a thin slip of white, an eye in the black starry sky in the last phase of a long, slow wink. I stopped in front of the barn and considered the swirls and knots that dotted the pine door. This place really had been a little piece of heaven for me, bone-weary reprobate that I was. I breathed in all the smells that I had grown to love, barn waste and hay, green grass and damp earth, and now the faint scent of apples. I slid the door open.

It was dark inside and smelled of oil and gas. It shouldn't have. I went into the stall that housed my bike and my foot kicked something metal. I backed out of the stall, found the light switch and turned it on. The bike was lying on its side, kickstand poking into the air, like roadkill in August. It was mangled. Pieces of it were scattered everywhere, and what wasn't broken was flattened, bent or twisted. I stared at the mess, blinking my eyes in confusion. Violence wasn't my father's style. His was a mental game. This wouldn't be his doing.

"Meri," I said to myself but then shook my head.

That couldn't be right either because she had been with me all day. I picked up the gas tank that was lying in a corner. It was mostly intact, leaking only small drops of gas through the feeder hose and in one other place where the weld had been broken. It was nearly empty. The rest of the gas was soaked into the straw. There was a deep dent in one side. I turned into the light. The dent was a crescent moon shape, eerily similar to a hoofprint. I heard a soft snort behind me and turned around. Sergeant was looking at me, his big eyes blinking softly, his ears swiveled forward. I could have sworn he was grinning. I looked at the tank and then I looked at him again.

"Sergeant, what have you done?" I asked him, nearly choking on the fear that rose up sharp inside me. His eyes opened wide, his ears drooped sideways and down. I dropped the tank and went around to his stall. The top door was open. The bottom door was open, too. I stepped inside. There were pieces of rubber and plastic all over his floor. He pawed the ground with a hoof and crunched what was left of a taillight.

"Oh, Sarge," I whispered.

He swung around and nudged me with his nose, pushing me hard against the wall. He stood there huffing at me, nostrils

131

flaring. A quick and sudden exhaustion rolled over me, a bone-deep fatigue that pulled at my limbs. I couldn't fight everybody. They were all demanding such different things. Even Meri. Even Sergeant. I couldn't do it. I wasn't brave enough. I wasn't strong enough. And now I couldn't run, either. I was screwed, well and truly. We were all screwed. Laurelvalley was screwed. Even Sergeant was screwed. He just didn't know it yet. I slid down the wall and sat in the hay leaning my head against the planks. Sergeant bent his head and nuzzled at me, huffing his faintly metallic breath into my face. I slid over sideways and lay in the hay. I couldn't do it. I couldn't be what anyone wanted me to be. Lover, daughter, mother, friend. I just couldn't do it. I pulled my knees in against my chest, curled my arms over my head and shut my eyes tight.

I was dreaming about the one time I went camping, an over-night wilderness trek with my college biology class to see the things that city people almost never see and mostly don't care to. I dreamt that one of my classmates struck flint to tinder and lit a small fire to roast some crickets, but I kept throwing log after log onto the flames until they were taller than my head and the thick smoke swirled all around us. It scratched at my throat and made me cough. It was the cough that woke me.

I opened my eyes. The wall in front of me was a solid mass of flames. "Shit," I yelled and scrambled into the corner. Over the crackle and roar, I heard shouts and frantic neighs from far off in the distance. I looked quickly around. Sergeant wasn't in the stall with me. I had never closed his door. I don't think I had closed the outside door either. A burning cinder drifted down and fell onto my hand. I shook it off with a yelp and looked up. Flames were starting to lick at the ceiling above me. The loft was packed to the rafters with well-seasoned hay. I'd put most of it there my-self. Smoke billowed from the cracks in the wood, dark and black. Tiny cinders began to rain down stinging my face and hands. I yelled and jumped to my feet. Fire slipped down my throat. Heat seared into my lungs and burned at my cheeks. My knees buckled and I fell coughing and choking. I couldn't catch my breath.

Ash and sparks swirled all around me like a glowing hot snow. I had to get out. I crawled toward the door, but the smoke was thicker that way. All around me, falling embers started smoldering in the hay scattered on the floor. I bent my head and could see between my legs the smoldering embers erupting into little flares of flame. No choice but to go forward. I crept along slowly, inching my way to the door. The smoke left an achingly bitter taste across my tongue as I struggled hard to breathe. My head turned dizzy and the ground underneath my knees started to buckle and sway. Heat seared across my back. I dropped to my belly and tried to keep moving. The smoke got thicker, and every breath I took sent jagged pains shooting through my chest. The world shrank to the move of a hand, the shift of a knee, the push of a foot. I made it out of the stall and into the walkthrough. I thought I made it at least as far as the door to the tack room, but the smoke was too thick. It fell from the ceiling, touched the floor and smothered me. The world swirled into gray and then faded to black.

I woke again to scorching bright pain. Every breath scraped my throat raw. The skin across my back felt swollen and tight. My cheeks stung. Nausea rose up and swept through me with a short, sharp spasm, clenching my muscles into hard knots. I rolled over and threw up. Hands held my shoulders and head. Voices spoke in sharp, urgent tones. "*Jesus, would you look at that.*" "*Get something on it, before she rolls over again.*" "*Josh, call this in. I'm going to start a drip.*" Someone grabbed my arm, and I felt a prick. My body slowly stopped its heaving. I stayed on my side with my face pressed into the dirt, focusing on the noises that surrounded me, the yelling and shouting, the roar of the fire, the rush of water, the hiss of steam, the crackle and pop of loud radio voices. Someone rolled me onto my back. The bright pain shot all through me, and I moaned a deep-chested sound that made everything hurt worse. Hands lifted me, set me down again and rolled me back onto my side. Something covered my nose and mouth, and I could breathe a little easier. The dark smoke that hovered all around me seemed to clear a little.

I opened my eyes to see strangers bending over me, sharp eyed with faces full of efficient concern. Flashing lights stained their hair blue, yellow and red. Taylor peered over a set of thin shoulders. Soot smudged his cheek as he looked down at me, upset and confused.

"Meri," I tried to say, but speaking made my throat burn and I coughed with harsh, rough spasms. Someone leaned over me, and I felt another prick in my arm. The coughing subsided. My body began to relax and my eyes to grow heavy.

"Meri," I called out to him. "Where's Meri?" I stretched out a hand to grab him, but the darkness welled up and covered me.

Chapter Six: GROWTH

There was light, then there was darkness again, and then a gray haziness, like smoke that filled my eyes. My body felt hot, tight and swollen, and then it felt cold and wet, then I was dry again and parched as the desert sands. Finally, the smoke drifted away on a light breeze that smelled sharply antiseptic. I listened and heard the soft shuffling of feet, the faroff sound of hushed voices. I opened my eyes. White sheets, a tan wall. I was lying on my stomach. My throat burned, and I tried to swallow. Bad idea. Things prickled inside. They stretched and pulled and slid down the wrong way. I coughed, or tried to, but my chest was too tight for me to do more than chuff. I tried to roll over. Needles of furious pain stabbed into my back. I groaned and lay still. Footsteps walked around the bed and Taylor stooped into my line of vision.

"Hey, you're awake," he said with a friendly smile that I instantly resented. "Don't try to turn over. Your back was pretty badly burned."

I tried to say something, but it just came out as a croak. Taylor put a straw to my lips and I drank.

I tried again. "Hurts," was all I could manage. The word was broken and distorted.

"Yeah, he said it would," Taylor said gently. "The doctor I mean. They're kind of limited in what they can give you for pain because of the baby." He pulled a chair up next to the bed and sat down. "The baby's okay, he thinks, but they're going to have to watch him real close, because of the smoke and all. You've got a good doctor working on you. Your father flew in the best." He grinned. It was his usual grin, but it was little shaky. "He's really pissing off the rest of the staff."

I didn't know if Taylor meant my father or the doctor. I wasn't sure if I was supposed to care. I decided not to. "Meri?" I asked.

His grin faded into seriousness. "She's going to be okay."

"Hurt?"

"Just a little." He looked away, and I waited. "Well," he said, not meeting my eyes, "truth be told, it looks a whole lot worse than it is. She has some small patches of third-degree burns and a few second-degree burns in some very strange places, but the smoke didn't hurt her as much as it did you. She's still here in the hospital, though, just down the hall."

"How?"

Taylor sniffed and shook his head. "I don't really know. Meri still won't talk to me very much. Old habits die hard, I guess." He lifted a hand to scratch at his stubble. It was almost a beard. "All I remember is waking up when Sergeant started having a connip-tion right outside the parlor window. That crazy dumb horse was standing on the front porch having a fit. I heard Meri shout, saw her run down the stairs and out the kitchen door." He laughed, a short, abrupt sound, and shook his head. "She was naked as a jay-bird with nothing but a blanket in her hands. It took me a second to realize that I wasn't having a dream, and then I grabbed the shotgun and ran after her. I guess I was thinking your father had come to cause trouble. But as soon as I opened the kitchen door, I saw that the barn was on fire. Flames were shooting out of the roof, and Meri was nowhere to be seen. I ran to the phone to call the fire department."

He shrugged with a little twitch of his shoulder. "I didn't know she had run in there after you. And before you ask, no, I don't know how she got you out. I don't know how she even knew you were in there. By the time I got back to the barn you were lying on the ground with a wet blanket over you and she was lying there next to you wearing nothing but ashes and soot." Taylor dipped his head, his mouth pressing into a hard, thin line. "You were both lying mighty still." He sniffed again and rubbed at his nose. "You oughtn't to scare a man like that."

"See her," I whispered harshly. Taylor's face went blank. I spoke again very carefully around the gravel and broken glass that lined my throat. "I want to see her."

Taylor shook his head slightly. "She looks a little rough, Bea. Maybe you should wait until the both of you are a little better."

I closed my eyes, slipped my hands underneath me and pushed. The pain that shot across my back was intense and nearly buckled my elbows.

Taylor put a hand to my shoulder and pushed me back down. "Hey, now, you can't get up. You're hooked to stuff."

"Have to see her," I said as all my energy slowly drained away.

Taylor puffed out a disapproving breath. "What is it with the women in this family? Y'all are more stubborn than a whole herd of hungry mules."

"See her. Please."

"All right," he said with an exasperated sigh. "She's more mobile than you are right now, even with the foot thing. Just lie still and I'll see if she's awake."

"Okay." I closed my eyes and fell asleep.

• • •

137

When I opened my eyes again, Meri was sitting in the chair next to my bed, her chin was in her hands and she was staring at me. Her whole head was swathed in bandages. Her forearms glistened with some sort of salve smeared over angry red blisters. A small line of black char ran just below her elbows. She smiled. I tried to smile back, but it must have looked ghastly. She put a finger to my lips and I kissed it. She leaned over and kissed my temple, brushing her lips lightly across my skin. I was surprised that it didn't hurt.

"The nurses made me promise not to let you talk too much," she said settling into her chair. "Your throat was slightly singed. On the inside, they said. You have a little damage to your vocal cords, but they should be all right if you don't work them too hard." She smiled again. "That's only just a little weirder than the burn on the inside of my right armpit or the ones between my toes."

"How?" I asked in my broken voice.

"Which one? The armpit or the toes?"

"Armpit."

"I have no idea." She gave me a wry smile. "I can't imagine what I was doing to get a burn under there. Waving at the parade, maybe? One guess is as good as the next."

"Toes?"

She smiled wider. "It seems I forgot to put my shoes on before I ran out of the house." She saw me looking hard at her and the smile faded. "I stepped on a few embers. Some got stuck between my toes. You have a few burns on your legs too where I dragged you through them. They're not too bad, but I'm afraid your blue jeans were ruined."

"Show."

She leaned back in the chair and held up a bandaged foot that was twice its normal size. "I'm supposed to keep it propped up, but it hurts more that way," she said, lowering her foot again. She was lying, but it wasn't worth pursuing. She would put it up when the nurses made her.

"Your head?" I asked.

She touched the place where her bandages dipped down over her forehead. "It looks like we might have nearly matching scars," she said. "Isn't that romantic?"

"Head, Meri," I demanded quietly.

Her hand dropped into her lap. "Part of the ceiling collapsed. I was standing in the doorway of the floor when something large and flaming fell on me. That's where I got these burns, too," she said showing me her arms.

"Standing over me?"

She reached over and put her hand to my mouth. "Don't forget what they said about talking too much."

I moved my hand slowly, inching my fingers across the sheet until I could touch her hand. I grasped her wrist and held it tightly.

"I'm sorry," I said against her fingers.

Her eyes narrowed just a bit. "Sorry about what, Bea?" she asked. "Sorry about burning my barn to ashes or sorry about trying to leave in the middle of the night without saying good-bye?" Her tone was wry, but her eyes held a deep hurt.

"You know?"

She nodded slowly, almost reluctantly. "I woke up when you went to the bathroom. I listened to you leave, heard you hopping over the squeaky floorboards. You crept quiet as a mouse down the stairs, but I heard the kitchen door open and close. I got out of bed and watched you from the window." She drew her hand away and I let go of her wrist. "When you went into the barn with your saddlebags, I went back to bed and buried my head under the pillow so I wouldn't have to hear your motorcycle start or hear you drive away." She scowled at the floor. "I really hate that sound."

"I'm sorry," I said again.

She shook her head sharply. "I stayed under the pillow for a long time. Then I heard Sergeant making an awful racket in the yard. I figured he was upset about you leaving, but then I realized that if I could hear Sarge, I should have heard your motorcycle, too. But I hadn't, so I got up to look. That's when I saw the barn burning."

"Why did you let me go?"

She didn't answer for a long moment and then she said, "You were doing what you thought was best." Her face was not pinched but it was pained. She looked at me with sad eyes. "It would've been wrong to try and make you stay. That would make me just one more person in your life trying to force you into doing something you didn't want to do." She folded her hands together and tucked them in her lap. "It would still be wrong to hold you, Bea, even now." Her eyes blinked rapidly. "When you get better, you can take my truck if you want to. If you still need it."

I blinked back at her. "Why would you do that?"

"I want you to do what you think is the right thing to do, even if I don't agree with you. You need to be able to live with yourself more than you need to be able to live with me."

"You don't think I should run anymore." My voice cracked, and Meri reached for a cup of water.

"No, I don't," she said, placing a straw between my lips. "I think you should try to face things head-on. I've been thinking about it a lot, you know, in the past few days." She took the straw away and touched the corner of my mouth where the water had dripped. "Your father's been bullying you all your life, and all your life you've been running from him as if his threats were promises." She put the cup down on the table. "But they're not. Just because he says he can do something doesn't mean he really can. There is some fairness in the world, you know."

"My father?"

"He's around here someplace," she said with a wave of her hand. "He's been making such an ass of himself trying to push around the hospital staff that they're starting to get a big kick out of tripping him up. They won't even let him in here to see you. Don't worry about him right now, Bea. You're in a safe place."

"Am I really?" I asked, looking at my empty hand lying on the sheet in front of me.

Meri gave me that quizzical tilt of her head. "What are you asking me?"

"You still want me, Meri, all burned like this?"

Meri leaned in closer, reached over and brushed her fingers through my hair. "Your face only has very minor burns on it, Bea. Your back will heal in time. You might not want to wear cocktail dresses anymore, but you're still a very beautiful woman."

"You?" I asked, looking at the bandages around her head.

She touched the white swath of gauze. "I wasn't a great beauty to begin with."

"Are to me," I said softly.

She looked at me, not quite believing. "Even now?"

"Cute in a turban." I tried to smile.

She grinned. "Why, thank you, sweet cheeks," she said with an exaggerated drawl, patting her bandages with the palm of her hand as if they were a fancy hairdo. "I'm so glad you like it." The grin faded from her face. Her hand sank slowly and she stared at it. "Bea, I need you to know something."

"What?"

"The doctors aren't sure if my hair will ever grow back in some places."

I made a noise, a small, tight groan. I loved Meri's hair, the shimmering gold blond of it as it spilled across her pillow, its tickling softness when it brushed across my skin. It was a source of pride for her too, a graceful balance to her angular planes.

"My fault."

Her hand covered mine. "It's not your fault," she said. "And if you can't deal with the way I look . . ." Her voice caught in her throat. "I mean, you're still welcome to take the truck for whatever the reason. You don't have to tell me why you're leaving."

"You want me to leave?" I asked, my words sounding more broken than ever.

Meri's face crumbled. She shook her head and mouthed the word no. No sound came out of her.

I turned my hand over underneath hers and laced our fingers together. "I'm not going to leave you again, Meri, no matter what. I need you to believe that I won't."

She wiped at her cheek with the sleeve of her hospital gown. "I don't know what that means, Bea."

"I want to stay with you." I swallowed painfully. "I want you to stay with me."

"I still don't understand," she said sounding confused. "Are you asking me to go with you?"

"No. I'm asking you to marry me."

Meri's eyes widened and she sat back in her chair. Our fingers came unlaced. She stared at me, unmoving, barely breathing.

I didn't like her silence. "I can't get down on one knee right now, but please believe that the question is sincere."

"I don't know what to say to that," she said. "It's not even legal in this state."

"Say yes anyway. We'll make our promises to each other, not to the state."

She shook her head slowly, not like she was saying no, but like she was trying to settle the idea in her brain. "Why do you want to do that?"

"I want you to believe me when I promise that I'll stop running away from things. I don't want you to worry anymore that you'll wake up one day and find me gone."

She raised a hand to her head and touched her bandages. "What about my hair?"

I wrinkled my nose at her. "I don't want to marry your hair."

"Bea, I'm serious," she said sternly. "It's very possible that I'll spend the rest of my life looking like the wrong end of an ugly dog."

"Not to me," I said moving my hand toward her. "Not to anyone, I think."

She shook her head and rubbed her hand across the bandages. "Can you honestly say that you would still find me attractive with only half a head of hair?"

"If I could move I'd show you how much." My longing for her rose above the pain, and I tried to let my face show it. "Right here, right now."

She smiled at me then, a lazy half smile that built slowly as want filled her eyes. "What would Aunt Beatrice think?"

"I don't think her poor heart could take it."

"No, not about that," she said with a shy wave of her hand. "About us getting married."

I grinned as best as I could. "We'll invite some celebrities. She'll love it."

Meri rolled her eyes and nodded. "Would we have some kind of ceremony where we invited friends and family, too?"

"Sure, if you want it that way."

"Would we have a rock band or something?"

"At the wedding?" I asked, not quite able to picture a rock band playing the wedding march.

"No," she answered with a grin. She probably couldn't picture it either. "I mean at the reception."

"Sure," I said. "If you want one."

She paused for a second, biting at her lip. "Would you dance with me, in front of everyone, even if I have lumpy scars on my head and no hair? Even if they all scowled at us and called us bad names?"

"Sam can put the pictures in the paper. We'll sell the video to the *Politics and Power* show."

She tilted her head and studied me very intensely. "You're serious, aren't you?"

"Yes, I am." Her eyes were a pale ice blue under her white bandages. "Meri, will you marry me?"

She leaned forward in her chair and kissed the corner of my mouth. "Yes," she said softly. "Yes, I will."

"Okay, then." I smiled and closed my eyes.

People were arguing and it was very annoying. Everything

had been so quiet for the last few days with me drifting around in a painful bliss. I woke often to find Meri's funny eyes staring at me, blue one time, gray the next, depending on the strength of the light or the color of her shirt. Or sometimes I would wake up to find Taylor asleep in the chair next to me, chin on his chest, his ball cap cocked crookedly atop his head, snoring softly. Most often, I woke to nurses politely poking and prodding at me, drawing gallons of blood, sticking tubes down my throat, salving my burns or rubbing cold ultrasound paddles over my stomach. They were still concerned about the baby, but there wasn't much to be done except keep an eye on it. It would be all right or it wouldn't, but saying that out loud made both Meri and Taylor frown pretty fiercely.

Even with all that, I rested better than I had in a long time. Something that lived inside me, wound like a tightly coiled spring, had eased. I couldn't say why because nothing had changed, really. My father was still running around being an atrocious pain in the ass. When he could get in to see me, which wasn't often, because the nurses wouldn't let him come in when Meri or Taylor were there, he kept trying to get me to sign papers that gave him legal authority to make decisions for me. Saying no to him got easier each time. Each time I remembered what Meri said to me. His threats were not promises. And so they weren't.

I shifted in the bed slightly, carefully rolling onto one shoulder to ease the pressure on my chest. Angry words buzzed like gnats around my ears. I turned my head to listen.

"I don't care who you are. It wouldn't matter if you were the president of the United States. You are not authorized to make decisions on her behalf." It was a woman's voice, a rough, smoky, tough as nails voice that I didn't recognize.

"I'm her father." My father answered in his senatorial tone, the one he used for shouting slogans and haranguing the masses. The two voices seemed well matched.

"It wouldn't change anything even if you were the pope," said the woman. "You're not authorized to move her. She's over twenty-one, an adult and responsible for her own decisions."

"I keep telling you people that she needs a better burn unit that what you have here."

"Not now she doesn't. She's stable and her back is healing quite nicely."

"It's peeling off. She's going to have scars. I don't want her to have scars." There was a slight rise in volume, a subtle shifting of pitch. My father knew he was losing this argument. Now the threats would come.

"It would peel even if she were in the Mayo clinic," the woman said calmly. "That doctor you've imported has done everything possible to minimize the scarring. He can't do anything more than what he's already done."

"I can't tell you how strongly I disagree." I couldn't see him from where I was, but I could picture him crossing his arms and lifting his chin, using his advantage in height to emphasize his disdain. "I'm telling you she needs a better facility, and if I have to have you removed from your position to make it happen, I will."

"You don't have that authority, Senator Torrington," the woman said in a tone of flat finality. "Even if you could, the decision still belongs to your daughter. If she decides that she wants to be moved, then she's welcome to it. But she's already made it quite clear that she doesn't want to be separated from her friend, and I don't hear you offering to move them both together."

"That other girl isn't my daughter." There was a shade of disgust in his voice, and it reminded me of the revulsion on Aunt Beatrice's face that time in the kitchen. It occurred to me that those two were more alike than either one of them would be comfortable with. I suddenly pictured my father wearing Aunt Beatrice's blue hair and started to giggle to myself.

"That other girl saved your daughter's life." The woman's voice was saying. "That other girl is someone your daughter cares for very much."

"Christ." My father's voice exploded and bounced off the

walls. "Does the whole world know about that?"

The woman laughed. It was a startlingly clear sound to come from such a rough voice, and I smiled to hear it.

"The part of the world that matters knows it," she said, "and the rest of the world will hear of it soon."

"What do you mean?"

"That hotshot doctor of yours heard opportunity knocking and called a press conference. It should be happening right about now, and since you're here, I'm guessing that someone forgot to tell you about it. I have no doubt the subject of your daughter and her friend will be thoroughly discussed, not mention the very mysterious fact that she's pregnant."

There was a long pause. "She really is?"

"She really is, Mr. Torrington. About three months or so."

I didn't hear him answer, but I heard heavy footfalls receding down the hallway. I recognized them as another storm coming, the thuds of his heels falling like thunder, the sharp slaps of his toes cracking like lightning. When I was young, that specific cadence of footfalls used to terrify me. I would run at their approach and hide in the hall closet, sitting behind the coats, burying my face in the soft furs until the storm had passed. It didn't mean anything at all to me now, just a strong wind blowing outside the windowpane.

I let my face sink back into the pillow and wondered at what a genius Meri was when she had the time to stop and think.

I sat on the edge of the hospital bed while Meri finished packing my bag. There wasn't much to it, just pajama bottoms, slippers, a toothbrush and some books. I could've packed it myself, but between the baby and the smoke, I had about zero energy. My back was much better. It was still tender in some places, but just itchy in all the others. I wasn't supposed to wear anything over it, except today they let me put a shirt on if I promised to take it off as soon as I got home. Meri promised the doctor with a gleam in her eyes that she'd make sure I did. She brought me one of her father's old sweatshirts that had a feed store logo with a picture of a bull on the front and room enough for two. It was more appropriate than she knew.

"Are you ready to go?" she asked.

"I think so," I said. My voice was still rough and maybe always would be, but I didn't mind because Meri thought it was sexy.

She grabbed her cane and limped over to sit next to me on the bed. The hospital discharged Meri a few days before, but they couldn't make her go home. She said there wasn't anything to go home to since Sergeant wasn't there. He disappeared the night of the fire and couldn't be found "for love nor money," as Taylor put it. Three days later, one of the cousins came across him wandering around in the east orchard, bloated, colicky and stumbling drunk from eating too many fallen and somewhat fermented apples. He was still at the vet's where, rumor had it, he was not being a model patient. We figured that meant he was feeling better and would probably pull through just fine.

Here at the hospital, Meri spent most of her time playing gin rummy with me, or, when I was sleeping, playing poker with the nurses until she cleaned them out of all their cashews and they didn't want to play anymore. After that, she would have me read poetry to her in my new sexy voice, the potential of which she was anxious to explore more fully once we got home.

"What's taking them so long with the wheelchair?" Meri asked, drumming one of her heels against the floor. Her other foot was still swathed in gauze from the surgery she had to keep her toes from fusing together.

"I don't know," I said. "Maybe they're having trouble finding one."

Meri snickered. A few nights ago, she wandered into pediatrics and got all the kids together for a wheelchair social. They had a great time of it until someone discovered that the more ambulatory kids had borrowed their wheelchairs from the emergency room. And there was another side of Meri that I hadn't known about. She liked kids and was good with them. It was fortunate that one of us was, I supposed.

"Do you have the instruction sheet that the doctor gave you?" I asked her.

"Yep, it's in your bag. You're going to have to wash my feet, you know."

"And you're going to have to wash my back."

Meri grinned. "I intend to wash your whole self, every inch, slowly and carefully."

I gave her my most lecherous wiggly-eyebrow look. "I'll change your bandages if you change mine."

"Now, who could resist an offer like that?" she said with a laugh and leaned over to kiss me on the cheek. Her lips lingered over my skin. "I sure wish they'd hurry with that chair," she whispered. "Why do you need one anyway? Why can't we just leave?"

"The hospital doesn't think it's dignified for patients to walk out on their own two feet."

Meri harrumphed. "Well, I'm glad we're getting out of here. One more hospital meal and I would've given up eating forever. Maybe we could swing by a pizza place on the way home."

"How are we getting home?"

Meri rolled her eyes. "Taylor wanted to come get us in the Duesenberg, but he hasn't painted it yet. He said it would look stupid to show up in something all rusty, but I can't imagine who he thinks would care. Plus it only has two seats and Aunt Beatrice wanted to come with him. I don't mind you sitting on my lap, but I draw the line at Auntie Bea."

The picture of Aunt Beatrice sitting on Meri's lap made me laugh, which started her to giggling, which made me laugh even harder and then that got her going, too. Meri snorted loudly and we near about fell on the floor. I held onto my ribs trying keep my back from jiggling around too much. Meri held onto her head with both hands. We sat there on the edge of the hospital bed and laughed until we both got the hiccups. It wasn't all that funny, but it sure felt good.

Meri shook her head and wiped her eyes on her sleeve. "Really, though, I don't understand why Auntie and Taylor are making such a big production out of this. Just because your father's got a schmancy car doesn't mean we have to have one too."

That sobered me and I felt the laughter fade. Meri didn't have the first clue about what was waiting for us just outside the hospital doors, and I hadn't yet found a way to tell her that she took seriously. I looked up at the television set that hung on the wall. It never occurred to Meri to turn hers on. She didn't know that the very second they wheeled me out of this room, both our lives would get considerably more complicated. As smart as she was, she could be so innocent about anything larger than Laurelvalley. She had no idea that we, she and I both, had gone national.

A doctor came into the room with a wheelchair, only it wasn't a doctor, but the woman with the smoky voice who turned out to be the hospital's administrator, and she wasn't alone. A whole gaggle of nurses, doctors and technicians lined the hallway to give us an escort to the lobby, or they would have, but there was a little bit of a scuffle in front of the elevator over who would get to ride in it with us. The administrator rolled my chair into the elevator herself and stood behind it with the nurses that had taken care of me fanned out around her. Meri stood at my side looking bemused as we rode down, not sure what all the fuss was about and thinking it unnecessary anyway. She wore an expression of friendly condescension right up until the time the doors slid open.

Flashbulbs popped. People were shouting, microphones waving, a whole flock of video cameras pointed in our direction. The entire lobby had people packed from one wall to the other. As the doors opened fully, the crowd surged forward and the noise level grew into a deafening din. This level of attention was new to me, but not very surprising, given the circumstances. I had expected something like it, but Meri stood frozen in the elevator, her mouth hanging open, eyes wide and staring. I don't think she was breathing. A phalanx of cousins, many I recognized as our best apple pickers, elbowed their way through the crowd and cleared a space for us. My chair began inching forward into the mob. I reached out and grabbed Meri's hand, pulling her stumbling along with me.

The cousins cleared a slow path to the door, but it was still like running the gauntlet. Meri, silent and stiff, limped with her cane beside my wheelchair. I smiled at everyone as politely as I could, saying, "We've no comment at this time," to a garble of questions that I wasn't really hearing. Meri, still in her turban of bandages, forearms swathed in gauze, looked like a spooked horse, eyes rolling, flanks shivering. A barrage of bulbs went off right in our faces, and Meri jumped. Someone screamed a question at her and stuck a microphone into her face. She ducked to avoid it, stumbled and fell. Her hands grabbed for the arm of the wheelchair, and it tipped over onto one wheel. I reached out to keep from falling, my hands clutching at her shoulders, and she reached for me. We met in an awkward half hug over the arm of the wheelchair, her hands gripping my arms tight. We both froze, our noses just an inch apart, and then she smiled at me sheepishly. I smiled back at her, slipped an arm around her neck and lifted a hand to touch her cheek. Flashbulbs popped in a hail of light. I didn't do it on purpose. It was just a natural gesture for me, but I knew it would make a great picture, one we could frame and hang on the stair wall.

Taylor and Aunt Beatrice were waiting for us at the curb in her ancient tan Buick sedan. I thought it made a nice contrast to my father's limousine. Plain versus fancy, modest versus extravagant. He left town just the day before in a frenzied hurricane of rage that had all his butt-kissers ducking and running for cover. None of his plans or threats had worked out. He couldn't get me released into his custody. He couldn't get his own imported doctor to attest to my mental frailty. He hadn't been able to stop the press conference. And he had not liked what the news outlets were saying about it all.

150

Meri was a hero, a shy knight in blue jeans who went riding into the flames on her noble steed to rescue me, the princess who didn't want to be a princess anymore. Not everything they said was true, of course. Nobody in their right mind would call Sergeant a noble steed, and the tabloids exaggerated the story quite a bit, especially the one that suggested it was really Meri who got me pregnant. But all the news outlets painted basically the same picture. I was the victim and my father the villain. Suddenly, in spite of his long incumbency and his efforts to galvanize the right wing hatemongers, my father's reelection campaign wasn't doing so well in the polls and his presidential bid was in a shambles. Aunt Beatrice was tickled pink, but I couldn't bring myself to care. My father never spared a thought for my dreams, and I found that I no longer cared about his. In the end, it didn't matter to me what people said about us, as long as they eventually left us alone. Meri, on the other hand, was just mystified by it all.

Meri burst into the kitchen, plastic grocery bags dangling from her arms. She dumped the bags onto the counter and banged a garishly colored newspaper down onto the kitchen table, making my teacup rattle in its saucer. "Bea, you've just got to read this one," she said, thumping the paper with a forefinger.

A sausage rolled across my plate and into the pancake syrup. I flicked the sausage out of the syrup, licked my finger and looked at the paper. There was a picture of a man with four arms on the front.

I wiped my finger on a napkin and picked up the paper to study the man's extra arms. They seemed to be growing out from his hips. It looked like he had lobster claws instead of hands, and I thought how useful that would be for opening champagne bottles and stiff cellophane packages.

"I'm glad to see we're finally off the front page." I put the paper down on the table.

Meri blushed a furious red. "I can't believe they published that picture," she said indignantly.

I lifted an eyebrow at her. "That coming from a woman who wanted to print a picture of me with pie all over my face and a cherry stuck up my nose?"

She put her hands on her hips. "That was different. It was funny. The picture these papers printed was nearly pornographic."

"Yes, well," I said, forking my sausage and scraping the syrup off against the side of the plate. "I distinctly remember asking you on that occasion if the blinds were closed."

"I thought they were." She sat down opposite from me at the table. "We're almost half a mile from the road. I can't imagine a telephoto lens capturing that much detail from that far away." She frowned and touched her head. "I didn't even have the wig on. No wonder they thought you were making love to an alien."

I studied her closely. Her blond gold wig was a pale imitation of her real hair. I thought it made her eyes seem all washed out. "I think you need to stop wearing that thing," I said. "Your hair is growing back just fine. It's just short and a little thin on one side."

"Yeah and that just happens to be the side someone took a picture of from all the way out on the road."

"He might not have been that far, Meri." I bit one end of the sausage and made a face. I couldn't stand the taste of sweet on savory. I put it down. "Remember Taylor catching that one guy lurking in the bushes outside the kitchen window?"

"Yes," she said hesitantly.

"And do you remember the guy skulking around in the pasture? The one that Sergeant nipped in the butt and then stamped on his camera?"

"Oh, yes," she said with a smile. "I remember that one. Isn't he suing us?"

"No, he was trespassing so he can't sue us," I said. "He's suing Sergeant."

"Poor Sergeant." Meri plucked the sausage off my fork and

began to nibble at it.

"Don't worry about him," I said, sipping my tea. "He's retained a very good lawyer."

Meri laughed. "I wonder how the lawyer feels about representing a horse."

"She's representing Sergeant, the noble steed and companion of Meri Donovan, hero of the hour. She's pleased as punch."

Meri reached across the table to snag one of my pancakes. Her eyes fell on the paper still lying there. "Oh, the article!" She picked up the paper and flipped through its pages. "Bea, you've just got to read it." Her eyes darted from page to page.

"Meri, you know I don't care what's in there."

"No, no. This isn't about us. Here it is." She folded the paper into quarters. "It's about your father. It says there's a rumor that he and your mother are getting divorced."

"What?" My teacup hit the table with a thud. "Give me that." I snatched the paper out her hand.

I read the article. It was short both in length and in details, but it was the first news of my father that we'd had since not long after he left the hospital in such a huff. I'd been expecting him to launch a counter media attack, something to paint himself as the grieving father, me as the wayward child and Meri as demon spawn from hell, but for the past month, he'd kept a very low profile and hadn't said a word to anyone about anything. It was such odd behavior for him that I was almost worried. I read the article through again and hoped that my mother wasn't bearing the brunt of his anger. I felt my cheeks grow hot. I hadn't even thought of her until now.

"Fuckin' A," I muttered.

"Bea!" Meri shook her head in disgust. "Taylor is such a bad influence on you. I wish you'd watch your language. The baby might hear you."

"Oh, please." I glared at her over the top of the paper. "The baby's still the size of my thumb, and I don't think she's bothered to grow ears yet."

"She's been in there for four months now, and that's plenty of time to grow ears." Meri began eyeing my pancakes again. "Besides, she or he is a lot bigger than your thumb. I think she's about the size of your whole hand."

"You've been reading too many books." I slid my plate over to her.

"One of us has to." She picked up a pancake and rolled it into a tube.

"Why? Women were having babies long before books about them were ever invented."

"Bea," she said seriously, "you're avoiding two issues here." Meri jabbed the rolled pancake in my direction. "First, it would be good for you to understand what's happening to your body, and second, I want to know how you feel about your parents getting divorced."

I put down the paper. "Okay, then. I understand that the baby's about the size of my hand and probably has ears. I also understand that I have to pee all the time, my boobs hurt when you squeeze them, and I can't button my jeans all the way. And furthermore, I think that my parents getting a divorce is by far the weirdest thing in this paper."

Meri dropped the pancake onto the plate. "Why didn't you tell me that before?"

"Which part? The pee, the boobs or the jeans?"

"The boob part. Why didn't you tell me that your boobs hurt when I squeeze them?"

"Because I like when you do it, and I didn't want you to stop doing it. You've already stopped kissing them. The poor things are starting to feel lonely and neglected."

She folded her arms across her chest and leaned back in her chair. "They're bigger than they use to be. I'm not sure what to do with them anymore."

"You don't have to do anything different. They're the same boobs. There are just a bit more of them."

"But it feels strange. Almost like you're nursing me."

"Trust me, Meri. I don't have any maternal feelings toward you."

"As far as I can tell, you don't have any maternal feelings at all."

She waited for me to answer, but I wasn't about to touch that one and spoil my whole morning. It was an argument we'd just recently started having after I told her what I'd planned to do about the baby while I was on the run. It shocked and offended her deeply. She said that she wouldn't have let me go if she'd known I was just going to throw it away. I didn't see it like that, and we hadn't yet found a point of compromise. I couldn't help what feelings I did or didn't have. I was acting in a mature and responsible way, taking good care of myself, which meant I was taking care of the baby, too. That was the best I could do. It wasn't fair for her to pile her expectations on me. She wasn't the one who had an alien life form growing inside her body.

Meri leaned forward and tapped the paper. "How come your parents getting a divorce is so weird?"

"Are you changing the subject?"

"Since you're avoiding one."

"Right," I said, scooting the paper closer to her. It was hard avoiding any subject that Meri thought was being avoided, but if she was willing to let it go then I wasn't going to argue. "I think the divorce is weird because my father owns my mother. He controls her so completely that I can't imagine him trading her off for someone he can't control quite as well."

"Maybe it's your mother who wants a divorce."

I picked up my tea, but it was stone cold, so I put it back down again. "My mother is a little mouse of a woman. I can't remember her ever saying anything more than 'yes, dear' to my father. I just can't picture her saying, '*Yes, dear, I read in the paper that our daughter's pregnant and having carnal relations with another woman. I think you handled the whole thing rather poorly, and by the way, I want a divorce.*'" I shrugged. "I just don't see it."

"Stranger things have happened," Meri said.

"We're living proof of that. And speaking of stranger things, what time is it?"

Meri glanced at the wall clock. "It's almost nine."

"Oh, darn it," I said very precisely and smiled when Meri rolled her eyes. "I have to get ready for work." I picked up my teacup and took it over to the sink. "I told Taylor I'd be in by eleven today."

"Bea," Meri started.

"Yes, dear?" I asked with a grin.

She picked up my plate and set it on the kitchen counter. "Do you really have to work with Taylor at the garage?"

"No. I don't have to. I like to. Fixing things makes me feel useful, and it's good for me to bring in a little money."

She shifted the plate to a new spot on the counter. "You could fix things around here."

I turned to look at her. "Do you need me to do more of the chores than I'm doing?" I asked her. "You want me to start cooking dinner?"

"God, no," she said with a shudder.

I stepped close to her and put my hands on her waist. "Do you miss me when I'm gone, or are you starting to get all jealous again?"

She stood stiffly and scowled at my chin. "You're having his baby. How am I supposed to feel when you run off and spend all day with him?"

"I'm having *our* baby, Meri, and he's hardly ever at the garage at the same time I am." I brushed a stray wig fiber off her cheek. "It's only three days out of the week, and it gives him the chance to make house calls for sick old farm trucks. Besides, he says he's still tail over teakettle for you, whatever the hell that means."

Her shoulders slumped. She leaned into me as best she could with my stomach poking into hers and put her head on my shoulder. I stroked the nape of her neck and she shivered.

"I'm sorry, Bea."

"I'm not." I pressed my cheek against her wig. "I kind of like you being all possessive of me."

"You're really strange," she said lifting her head.

I gently slid her wig off and set it on the counter. I ran my hands over her head. Her hair, about a half inch long now, tickled my palms. There was still a raw patch of scalp near the top of her head that had no hair and probably never would again. It was still beautiful to me. "I think you're the most gorgeous woman in whole world, Meri." I leaned in to kiss the burn scar that trailed off into her hair.

"Prove it," she said, sliding her hands into the back pockets of my jeans. They weren't buttoned or zipped and they sagged across my hips.

I slid my arms around her and pressed my palms flat across her spine. "Are the blinds closed?"

"Who cares?" she asked, tilting her head and kissing me lightly, her mouth nibbling at mine, pancake and sausage flavors still on her tongue. The press of her mouth set my toes to tingling, and I kissed her with an eagerness that melted her against me. "What about Taylor?" she whispered.

"Taylor can wait. What about the groceries?"

"Oh, damn!" she said, pulling away from me. "Your ice cream's going to melt."

I pulled her back. "The ice cream can wait."

She laughed. "It couldn't wait an hour ago."

"You should have kissed me then," I said, circling my hands around her waist. "I would have forgotten all about it."

"I'll remember that for next time." She tugged on my jeans. They fell off my hips and pooled around my ankles. Her hands slid into my underwear and rubbed across my butt. She squeezed and sank to her knees, pulling my panties down with her. I rubbed my hands over her head, her hair whispering against my palms. She leaned forward and I gasped.

Chapter Seven: MISTLETOE

"There are no such things as fashionable maternity clothes," I said to myself standing naked and shivering inside the closet, fresh and still damp from my morning bath. Christmas was just a few weeks away, and I had nothing to wear to any of the parties that Meri and I were invited to. We received a zillion invitations, mostly from people I'd never heard of, for dinners, galas and balls, but we were only going to two of them, Taylor's Garage Shop Hop for New Year's and Aunt Beatrice's Family Informal on Christmas Day. I thumbed my way through the clothes hanging on my side of the closet, scowling at the scant pickings. There wasn't anything I wanted to put on. I fingered a favorite pair of blue jeans that I hadn't been able to slide on over my bulging backside for about three weeks now. Maybe I could do a Scarlet O'Hara and wrap myself in a curtain. I looked over my shoulder at the curtains hanging in the bedroom window. They were very floral. Ick.

I thumbed through Meri's clothes and picked out a pair of black stretchy sweatpants and a red extra large sweatshirt with the faded logo of some football team crumbling on the front. It was better than the muumuus I'd be forced into in another month or two. I was not liking this pregnant thing, and the more bloated my body became, the more I began to resent it. I felt big and slow and stupid. My appetites weren't my own, and I didn't like being controlled by the fluttery thing in my belly. I couldn't ever tell if I was hungry, horny or just had gas.

I heard the bedroom door open and close. A waft of chilly air blew across my butt. Meri stuck her head into the closet. "Hey, Bea, come downstairs and give me a hand with the decorations." She stopped and stared at me. I turned around to give her the full frontal and had to smile at the look on her face. "Better put some clothes on first," she said, her voice going low and husky, "or we'll never get anything done."

My smile faded. "I don't have any clothes." I waved the sweatpants at her. "I'm wearing your fat clothes, and I won't even fit into those pretty soon."

"I suppose you could run around naked," she said with something close to a leer. "I wouldn't object."

"But it's cold." I crossed my arms and shivered. "I hate this, Meri. I don't like what's happening to me. I'm getting so big that my underwear doesn't fit anymore."

Meri stepped inside the closet. "Bea, I told you we could go shopping for clothes anytime you're ready."

"I don't want new clothes," I said with a sniff. "I want my old clothes. I want to be like I used to be."

Meri grabbed the sleeve of a shirt hanging nearby. She used it to dab at the corner of my eye. "You've just got to deal with it for a few more months," she said and tickled my chin with the shirt cuff. "I'm right here to help you."

I pushed her hand away from my face. "It's easy for you. You're not walking around like a bloated walrus."

Her lips twitched as she tried not to laugh. "You're not that big yet."

"Yet, Meri. This is only going to get worse," I said. "I don't want to do this. Too many things are changing."

She stepped into me and laid her hands on my stomach, rubbing soft round circles over my belly. Her hands slid up and cupped my breasts. She ran her thumbs over cold-puckered nipples. "Here's something that won't ever change," she said gently.

I dropped the sweats and leaned into her hands. She squeezed and I gave a little gasp. It hurt in such a wonderful way.

"Touch me," I said, leaning in harder against her hands.

She kissed me lightly, soft lips, the slight tip of her tongue and then she pulled away. "We can't, Bea. Taylor's coming over in just a little while. He's bringing some of the cousins to finish clearing away what's left of the barn."

"Please," I said, pulling her against me and nuzzling at her neck. "Just a quickie."

Meri laughed against my cheek. "Since when have we ever been able to have a quickie?"

She was right about that. Hours could disappear at the touch of her hands. She kissed me again and sank to her knees. At first, I thought she had changed her mind, but she picked up the sweatpants and held them out for me to step into. I gave her another little groan, one of disappointment and frustration. She watched me as I slid my feet into the leg holes.

"Your underwear really doesn't fit anymore?" she asked tugging the pants up to my thighs.

I finished pulling them up and settled them low on my hips, the waistband catching me on the down slope of my protrusion. "Nothing fits me anymore."

She pursed her lips and nodded. She leaned forward and kissed my bellybutton. A quick flick of her tongue sent shivers skittering all over my skin. "We're going shopping tomorrow." She picked the sweatshirt up off the floor, stood and handed it to me.

"You hate shopping."

"I hate you being unhappy more than I hate shopping."

I slipped the sweatshirt on over my head. "Maternity clothes are ugly."

"Why don't you wait until you've tried some on before deciding to hate them all?" Meri tugged on the hem of the shirt, pulling it over my stomach.

"Do you always have to be the voice of reason?"

She gave me another kiss. "No. Only when you're being unreasonable. Will you come down now and help me decorate the tree?"

"Of course," I said. "I'm not about to leave the icicles up to you. You have no sense of proportion."

Meri had set the tree in the parlor. It was a beautiful live fir with thick green branches and a crisp evergreen smell. I stood in front of it tossing the tinsel in the air in the hopes that when it floated down it would hang naturally. It wasn't working, and I had to keep picking clumps of it out of the branches. I got tired of Meri snorting and rolling her eyes at me and told her to go do something more useful. She thought about it for a minute and then said she was going to go get more stuff from the attic. I didn't think the tree needed anything else, it was already loaded with ornaments and garlands, but I was glad to get her out of the room for a few minutes.

Taylor had already come over with about two dozen cousins in tow. Every one of them, girl and boy, was wearing a ball cap and a tool belt. They didn't stop to chat but got right to work tearing down the burned remains of the barn. There wasn't much of it left standing after the insurance people got done poking through it, just a part of one wall with a chunk of the roof still attached. The rest of it was burned to cinders. The remains of my poor bike were still in there somewhere, except for the charred gas tank that the insurance lady impounded as evidence. I think she just wanted a souvenir, but Meri told me to stop being so sour about it. We were lucky that they blamed the fire on Sergeant and his sparking horseshoes because, strange as that sounded, it was covered by her policy.

I gave up on the tinsel and went into the kitchen to watch the cousins from out of the window. In spite of the chill, they were having a great time going at it with axes, sledgehammers, chain saws and one pint-sized bulldozer. It looked like a lot more fun than decorating, but both Meri and Taylor wouldn't let me lift anything over five pounds. The two of them, being overly concerned about my delicate condition, would pitch a collective fit if I went out there and tried to swing a sledgehammer. I twitched the curtain back farther and watched Sergeant pace the temporary fence. It was just steel posts and chicken wire that we circled around the gap where the barn used to be. It would probably hold all right as long as he didn't try to scratch his butt against it. He tossed his head, flipped his tail and tried to nip anyone who came too close to the fence. He was making it perfectly clear to everyone that he was unhappy with all the noise they were making. The silly horse had been insufferable since winning his lawsuit.

"Hey, Bea, where'd you go?" I heard Meri calling from the parlor.

"I'm in the kitchen," I said. "Do you want me to bring you anything?"

"No, I want you to come here and help me go through these things."

I went back to the parlor where Meri sat surrounded by dusty boxes. She had a smudge on her chin and cobwebs stuck in her stubble. Her hair was still only about an inch and half long, but she had stopped wearing the wig. I think she was far prettier without it.

"What's all this?" I asked.

She was rummaging around inside a huge box marked X-MAS in bold red and green sparkly letters. She sneezed and wiped at her nose.

"They're house decorations. You know, for the shelves and the mantle and the front door and stuff. I haven't pulled any of this out since the year before my parents died." She gazed into the box with shiny eyes. I knew she would want me to think that it was just the dust, so I didn't react to it. She reached a hand in and rustled through the tissue paper. "I wasn't sure about dragging it out because I don't know if any of this stuff is good enough."

"Good enough for what?"

"For you," she said. "I know you're used to your holidays being far more elegant than this." She held up a stuffed Santa doll wearing a crocheted hat and vest with a beard of curly white yarn. Wire-rimmed glasses, made out of a bent paperclip, sat sewn onto his nose.

"Meri, I don't know where you get such ridiculous ideas." I took the doll out of her hands. "This is cute. Why would you think it wasn't good enough for me?"

She waved her hand at the boxes. "All these decorations are homemade. There isn't anything here store-bought."

"That just makes it all the cuter. So, who made this one?" I asked as I straightened out Santa's glasses and brushed my fingers through his beard.

She blushed and bent over the box. "I did. Well, my mom did the crocheting and I did the stuffing and sewing." She shrugged and rubbed at her cheek. "It was just something we did. She would have a Christmas project for us every year, and we'd work on it together." She looked around at all the different boxes. "There's a gingerbread house in here somewhere. Made with real gingerbread. My dad shellacked it so the mice wouldn't eat it." She reached behind her and picked up a large flat box. She opened it, reached inside the plastic wrapping and pulled out a wreath with intricately woven deep green holly leaves, bright red berries and a gold bow tied around a large plastic candy cane. She held it up to me.

"Meri, that's beautiful," I said, though I wasn't actually crazy about the plastic candy cane. Meri was still very sensitive about anything related to her parents, and I had learned a lot about discretion from mine.

"You don't mind it going on the front door? I thought it might be too tacky for you."

"No, of course I don't mind. Did you and your mom make that?"

She nodded and turned it around, pointing to a little tag at the back. "We made it when I was about thirteen."

"And you kept it all these years?"

She nodded again and set the wreath back in its box. I looked down at the Santa and then at the wreath. I couldn't imagine what it was like having a mother to talk to and who would do things with you. It seemed right though, that a mother and her daughter should spend time together like that. I thought of the baby growing inside me, about five and half months now, with ears and a nose, little hands and tiny toes as Meri kept me informed in her weekly progress reports. It occurred to me right then that this baby was going to be a real person, one who deserved a real mother. I wasn't sure what a real mother was supposed to do, but I knew I wasn't up to the task. I hoped Meri could be mother enough for the both of us, but somehow that didn't seem fair to her or the baby.

"Meri, is the Christmas project thing something that you'll want to do with our daughter when she's born?"

She smiled at me, sad and happy at the same time. "Why don't we all do it together? We'll make it a family project."

I smiled too, touched by her sadness, and set the Santa on the mantle. If Meri wanted us to be a family, I would try my best, in spite of myself. "Is there a Mrs. Claus in there somewhere?"

Meri shoved the box over to me with her foot. "All the reindeer and Rudolph, too."

I sat on the couch, pulled the box over to me and started rummaging through the tissue paper. The kitchen door slammed, and I lifted my head at the sound.

"Yoo-hoo, anybody home?" Aunt Beatrice called from the

kitchen.

I brushed the tinsel off my sweatshirt and ran quick fingers through my hair while Meri grimaced and swiped at her face with her sleeve, but it was more out of habit than anything else. We both enjoyed Auntie's visits, within limits. We hadn't seen very much of her lately and were overdue.

"We're in the parlor, Auntie," Meri called out to her.

Aunt Beatrice and her blue hair shuffled into the parlor, and plopped herself down in the wingback chair. She slumped back and gazed around the room.

"What a lovely tree," she said, "if just a tad clumpy with the tinsel. You know if you just throw a handful of it into the air it'll hang more naturally."

I suppressed a sigh but Meri raised an eyebrow. Auntie was wearing slacks and a powder blue sweater with snowflakes on it, which, in itself, was unusual, even though the ensemble did match her hair. She usually dressed in her Sunday finest to go visiting. But more than that, she was such a strong believer in presence and decorum that seeing her shuffle, plop and slump was really very surprising.

"Would you like some tea, Auntie?" Meri asked getting up from the floor.

"No, thank you, dear. I hope you don't mind me popping over like this. I know you prefer that I call first, but I knew Taylor was going to be over here, so I assumed it would be safe."

Meri's eyebrows went up so high they would have disappeared into her bangs if she had still had any. Auntie had never before made even an indirect reference to the nature of our relationship unless it was in the vaguest of terms to tell us how much she disapproved.

Auntie waved a hand at Meri. "Sit, child, sit. No need for you to stand there like a stop sign."

Meri blinked at her for a moment and then sat back down. "What can I do for you today, Auntie?"

"Not a thing, my dear. I didn't come here to see you."

165

I steeled myself for the inevitable. I could feel a mandatory dinner invitation coming my way, and I really didn't have a thing to wear. After Thanksgiving, her invitations began to taper off since by then most of the excitement was already over. Even the paparazzi skulking in the bushes finally went home. The world had moved on to new faces and fresher stories, but Auntie still liked to show me off from time to time.

"What can I do for you, Auntie?" I asked, unwrapping Dasher and Comet from their tissue paper. I didn't recognize them. The saddle blankets had their names sewn on them.

"Oh, I just came over to ask if you knew that your mother was missing."

My hands fumbled and I dropped Comet onto the floor.

"I'll guess that means no," Auntie said with pursed lips and a slight shake of her blue head. "I declare, you girls really should read a newspaper now and again."

"What do mean by 'missing'?" I asked her.

"Missing, my dear, as in gone, disappeared, unable to be located, vanished, gone astray, misplaced, et cetera." Auntie was very good at crossword puzzles.

"For how long?" I asked. Meri and I hadn't picked up a paper in over three weeks. There hadn't been any more news about their divorce, so we assumed it hadn't been true.

Auntie rolled her eyes and bobbed her head like she was counting the days. "About two weeks now, I'd say."

"Oh my god," I said hugging Dasher to my chest. I had a sudden and clear vision of my father finally snapping and doing something truly unthinkable.

The thought scared me until shame and guilt flooded through me in much larger proportions. I hardly ever thought about my mother, anymore. I couldn't even remember what she looked liked. Dark hair and pale skin, like me, though my skin wasn't very pale anymore, but I couldn't picture her face. I couldn't remember the color of her eyes or the shape of her nose. Meri reached over the boxes and touched my arm.

I stood. "Meri, I've got to go. He'll talk to me. He'll tell me what he's done and where she is now."

"Who'll talk to you? Where do you have to go?" Meri asked, standing up with me.

"I have to go to California to talk to my father. He's done something bad," I said, clutching at her shoulder. "I just know it."

Meri stepped around the boxes and held on to my arms. "Bea, calm down. You're jumping at shadows."

"No, Meri, I'm not. You don't understand. My mother's not a strong person. She's just a little mouse. If she's missing then my father will be the one who's misplaced her." She would be resting in a place that was neither quiet nor restful. I clutched at Meri's arms. "Don't you see? He'll be the only one who'll know where she is."

"I know where she is," Aunt Beatrice said, sitting straighter in the chair, looking terribly smug. "And I wouldn't be so quick to judge her strength, if I were you, Collier. It takes all kinds to run this world, and sometimes there's more courage to be found in the heart of a mouse than there is in the paws of a lion." She patted at her hair and smiled. "I think I read that in a book somewhere."

Meri and I both turned to look at her.

"Are you saying that everyone else in the world thinks Bea's mother is missing, but you know where she is?" Meri asked incredulously.

Auntie Beatrice nodded with a prim little smile.

"Where is she?" I asked.

"She's sitting outside in the car."

"What?" I sat down again, abruptly. "Out where? In what car?"

"She's outside in your driveway," Auntie answered, "sitting in my car." She smiled softly. "Your mother wasn't sure you'd want to see her, so I told her I'd come in first to test the waters."

"Not want to see her? Why would she think that? Why

wouldn't I want to see her?"

"Why would you want to?" Aunt Beatrice asked with a sharp look in her eye that reminded me very much of Meri when she was in a mood.

"Oh," I said, understanding.

"What's she doing out in your car?" Meri asked.

"That, dear heart, is a very long story." Aunt Beatrice stood. "It's one I think she should tell you herself. Do you want to hear it? I can just go fetch her."

Meri looked over at me, but I didn't answer. I got up, shoved Dasher into Meri's hands and went into the kitchen. From out the window, I could see Auntie's old tan Buick parked in the drive. There was someone sitting in the passenger seat. A woman. Her head was turned. She was watching the cousins who had lit a small bonfire of charcoaled planks and were roasting hot dogs and sausages on long sticks over the flames. The woman had a round chin and a small upturned nose. Yes, I remembered that now. I opened the kitchen door, and the chill December breeze blew through my sweatshirt. Goose bumps popped up all over, but I'm not so sure it was from the cold. I stepped off the porch and walked over to the car.

My mother turned her head. Her eyes were gray, like Meri's were when the lights were dim or when she wore a dark blue shirt. She stared at me as if she wasn't sure who I was. She looked at my hair, at the scar on my forehead and then her eyes dropped down to my stomach. I ran my hands over the swell of it. Her mouth made a little "o" and her hand pressed against her chest. I leaned forward and opened the car door. She got out slowly. I had forgotten how much taller I was than her. The top of her head only came to about my shoulder. When I was younger, people used to say that we looked alike. I bet we didn't look anything alike now. Her hair was still long and her skin still pale. She seemed dangerously thin and fragile.

Her chin tilted up and her eyes flickered over my face. I had changed so much since she saw me last, with my skin suntanned and my body bloated.

"Collier," she said. It sounded almost like a question.

"Mother," I answered, but mine was really a question too. She seemed to understand what I was asking, and tears welled in her eyes.

"Not much of one, I guess," she said, her eyes jumping between the two of mine.

"No," I agreed. "Not much of one."

"I'm sorry, Collier," she said, her eyes dropping to my chin.

I shrugged. "You did the best you could."

She nodded but then shook her head. "I didn't do anything for you."

"You didn't do anything to me, either. Maybe that was the best you could do."

"I should have taken you and gone away somewhere." Her eyes faded out of focus. "I dreamed about it often enough."

"Why didn't you?" It wasn't an accusation. I was only curious.

She blinked rapidly. "I didn't know where to go. Everyplace I knew was worse than the place we were. It never occurred to me to look for a place I didn't know."

"You made it all the way out here."

Her eyes sharpened and rose to meet mine. "I followed you."

I looked away from her briefly as my heart did a funny skip. "That feels kind of strange."

She nodded her head. "A mother should show her daughter the way, not the other way around."

"Is that what mothers are supposed to do?" I asked, touching my stomach.

Her eyes dropped to my hands. "I don't know."

We stood in silence, my mother staring at my hands, then her hands, her shoes, the ground, the sky, at anything but me. She stood with an uncomfortable stiffness, a waiting restlessness.

"Mother." She turned her head in my direction. "I don't fault you for anything. Not anymore."

Her eyes closed for a second and she took a deep breath. "You're more forgiving than I."

"Don't credit me for more than I'm worth," I said shaking my head. "I'm not being altruistic. It's just that I understand what it is to be given nothing but bad choices." I touched her lightly on the arm. "I lived in fear of him, too."

She looked up at me then with her eyes squinted. "You've grown, Collier."

I looked down at myself. "Sideways and out. I look like the broad side of a barn."

"You look beautiful to me."

She reached out a hand to touch my cheek and I stood very still. I couldn't recall her ever touching me as a child. I'd always run to the nanny-du-jour for comfort until I learned to stop asking for comfort. Her fingers felt strange on my face. I think my face felt strange to her fingers. She drew back her hand and rubbed them together.

"I'm so sorry," she said, her chin quivering. The weight of my twenty-four years hung off her words, dragging at her voice, filling it with debris, the refuse of our broken family.

"So am I," I said, my voice catching. I took a step forward and gently put my arms around her. She stood stiffly and then her whole body seemed to sigh. She leaned her head against my shoulder and slid an arm around my waist. It was an awkward hug at best, with her short stature and my protruding stomach, but it was the first one I could remember. For a first, it was perfect.

Meri busied herself making tea and a plate of small cucumber sandwiches. When I introduced them, my mother shook her hand warmly and thanked her for being so good to me. Meri blushed scarlet and stammered out some reply. It surprised me, too. Aunt Beatrice sat herself at the kitchen table, her back to the refrigerator, and surveyed the room with a smug, self-satisfied expression.

170

Meri brought the tea and sandwiches to the table and we all sat. Aunt Beatrice put a sandwich on her plate, but the rest of us kept our hands in our laps. Meri scooted her chair closer to me and pressed her leg against mine. I reached under the table and put my hand on her knee. Aunt Beatrice sniffed and poured herself a cup of tea. My mother looked at us with a curious expression on her face.

"You're happy here, Collier," she said.

I glanced at Meri and nodded. "Yes, I am. Things are simpler here. Not easier, just less complicated."

Meri coughed into her hand. I shot her a stern look but then shook my head and smiled. She was right, as always. We had made a huge mess out of everything. Things really weren't that simple anymore.

"Does my being here complicate things?" my mother asked.

"I don't know, yet," I said. "It depends on what you've brought with you."

"Nothing, I think. I've been staying with Ms. Donovan," she said with a nod of her head in Aunt Beatrice's direction. "I've been there for a little over a week now, and we've not heard a peep out of your father. We know from the papers that he's filed a missing person's report, but my disappearance wasn't nearly as spectacular as yours, and the papers aren't as interested."

"You don't think he's out looking for you?" Meri asked her. "Because he's sure to look here."

Fear flashed in her eyes, but, as fast as it came, it was gone again. "I don't know. He's changed." She looked over at Meri and up at her hair.

"He didn't seem very changed to me," I said, remembering him at the hospital.

"No," she said, "not at first. He was so very angry when he first came home. He started phoning people, calling in favors, sending Wesley on mysterious errands all around the country. I don't know what he had planned, but I'm sure it wasn't nice."

Aunt Beatrice tsked and reached for another sandwich. Auntie put one on my mother's plate as well and poured her a cup of tea.

"Thank you," she said to Auntie and smiled wistfully as she looked around the table. "The newspeople started saying such nice things about you, about all of you, and painting him to be quite the ogre. That was what was different. He has lost battles before, but he's never been the villain. He's always been able to talk himself into the media's good graces, but that wasn't happening this time." She paused, toying with the sandwich on her plate.

"Go on, dear," Aunt Beatrice said, "in for a penny, in for a pound."

My mother nodded and swallowed. "His people stopped responding to him. He wasn't getting what he wanted. Public opinion was backing you, and then when his own party started lining up against him, he went insane." She shuddered and touched her shoulder like she was remembering a distant pain.

I felt Meri stiffen next to me, and Aunt Beatrice tsked again. My mother seemed to shrink down in her chair, but then she lifted her chin and sat up straight.

"All the raging died suddenly," she said "and he started brooding. He shut himself away in his study and didn't talk to anybody for days." She folded her hands and tucked them into her lap. "I wasn't sure what scared me the most, the wild explosions or the silent scheming. He wasn't talking to me. But then, he never did. I don't think he thought I had any opinions." She blushed. "I'm not sure that I did. I was so used to him telling me what I should think." She looked at me, her eyes clear and bright. "I read everything the papers said about you, Collier. I started thinking about how brave you were, and I wondered where it came from because your father's bold, but he's not at all brave, and I was taught from the cradle to be scared of everything. You were never scared of anything."

I shook my head. "I was scared of everything, too. It was just that at some point I got more angry than afraid."

172

Meri reached behind my chair and put her arm around my shoulder. Aunt Beatrice pursed her lips but didn't say anything.

My mother reached for her teacup and took a careful sip. "Yes, that was exactly it," she said. "I read all those things about you and I began to admire you like you were some hero in a book. I wanted to get to know you, and then I realized that I could have. I could have all along, but I never did." She set the cup down carefully in its saucer. "Your father had such clear plans for you, and I didn't dare interfere. But I should have, and the more I thought about it, the angrier it made me, at him and at myself."

"What did you do?" I asked.

"I . . . I'm afraid I had been drinking a little. It made me, well, not less afraid, but less mindful of the consequences. I marched into his office and asked him for a divorce. Right in front of Wesley, too."

Meri nodded. "That must be where the papers got it from."

"I wouldn't put it past him," I said with a huff. I looked back at my mother. "So, what did he say?"

My mother's eyes widened a little. "He just stared at me like he didn't know who I was and never said a word. I got scared all over again. I sat in my rooms waiting for the retribution, but days passed and it never came. I thought about you a lot, and it suddenly occurred to me that it was stupid to sit around waiting for the sword to fall. What I needed to do was to step out from under it. I packed a bag and took a taxi to the train station." She touched the handle of her teacup. Traced the circle of it with a fingertip. "There wasn't anywhere else for me to go but here. I wasn't sure you'd want me around, but . . . I called Ms. Donovan from the station."

"She remembered me from my picture in the paper," Aunt Beatrice said, sipping at her tea with a pleased little slurp. "Remember, Meri, the day I picked you girls up from the hospital?"

"Yes, Aunt Beatrice, I remember," Meri said with a smile. Aunt Beatrice had kept a scrapbook of pictures and articles and delighted in reliving her adventure over iced tea and buttermilk biscuits with anyone who would sit still for an hour.

"And we've been having a grand old time ever since. Isn't that right, Elizabeth?"

My mother smiled at her, too. It was soft and kind. "Yes, we have. I'm learning a lot of new things about the world." Her eyes fell. "And some new things about myself, too." She took a deep breath and let it out slowly. "Collier, I know it's too late for me to try and be a mother to you now, but I would like for us to try and be friends."

I looked at my empty plate. I had no idea if such a thing were possible, being friends with your mother. I wasn't sure if I wanted to be friends. Maybe I still wanted a mother or someone who could show me how to be one.

"Do you need a place to stay, Mrs. Torrington?" Meri asked, her hand squeezing my shoulder. "I mean, I know Auntie's house is pretty small compared to what you're use to. We have the whole guest wing that's empty right now. You're welcome to it if you'd like."

My mother smiled warmly at her but shook her head. "Thank you, but no." She turned her smile to Aunt Beatrice. "Ms. Donovan has agreed to let me rent her upstairs rooms from her until I decide where I'd like to settle."

"I'm getting too old to tromp up and down all those stairs," Aunt Beatrice said, nibbling delicately at her second sandwich.

I pressed my knee tighter against Meri's. "Mother, forgive me for asking, but do you have enough money?" Surely, my father had cut her off, too, just as soon as she left. I had no idea how good she was at planning ahead, or even if she did.

"Do you?" she asked with an odd look.

I felt myself pink a little. I didn't really, except for the little bit I made working at the garage. All the money I had left had been inside my saddlebags, and now there was nothing left of it but little bundles of ash. Paper burns just as easily as heart pine and hay. "I don't have much," I told her, "but Meri's not been charging me rent or anything."

"Bea pulls her own weight around here," Meri said a little defensively. I pushed at her knee, and she stepped lightly on my foot.

My mother smiled shyly. "You may have more left than you realize. A good bit of the Torrington money belongs to you. All of the initial capital your father used to invest came from my family. It's still held in trust."

I blinked at her. "But Daddy always said . . ." My voice trailed off as I struggled to recall the words he used. "No, he never actually said that he earned it. He only implied and let me draw my own conclusions."

"It's his greatest gift," she said softly.

"And my credit cards," I asked, "they haven't been cut off?"

"They're paid from the trust. As long as you're not overextended, they can't be cut off."

"And my allowance?"

She gave a slight shrug of her shoulders. "It came from the trust. You're over twenty-one, you know, Collier. It's not an allowance anymore. It's a dividend. That trust money belongs to you."

I turned to Meri, wide-eyed, thinking of all the scrimping we'd had to do to pay doctor bills and such. Meri's parents hadn't left her poor, but babies did tend to put a dent in your savings, especially babies that had been roasted and smoked. Meri was looking down at her lap, and didn't meet my eyes. I squeezed her knee, but she dropped her arm from my shoulder. She stood abruptly and reached for the teapot. "I'm going to warm this up," she said and moved away from the table. Her voice was flat and there was a stiff set to her shoulders. I looked a question at her, but she kept her back turned as she fiddled with the stove.

"Collier," my mother said, "Ms. Donovan tells me that you haven't bought any new clothes yet. Would you like to go shopping with me tomorrow?"

I smiled at her brightly, but before I could answer, the kitchen door opened with a puff of cold air. Taylor and the gang tromped inside filling the kitchen and the rooms beyond with their loud voices and laughter. They carried the smell of burning pine and crisply cooked sausages in on their jackets while they tracked soot from the soles of their boots across Meri's clean floor.

They nipped from silvered flasks to take the chill off while they jostled and bumped elbows and hunted through the refrigerator for slices of bread, spicy mustard and dill relish. I introduced Taylor to my mother, who shook his hand shyly. He sat next to her, offered her a beer from the cooler and a charred hot dog from a passing plate. I'm not sure, because the kitchen was so full, but I think I saw her laugh. Meri scowled and banged things around on the counter until the collective jokes and good cheer of twenty plus cousins jiggled a smile out of her. Someone handed her a flask. She took a swig and spluttered and coughed, blinking away tears while someone else slapped her on the back and laughed at her.

Aunt Beatrice sat straight in her chair, nibbled on a sausage and sipped her tea through tightly pursed lips, shaking her head and tsking. She leaned in closer to my mother. "Young people these days just have no sense of decorum."

As night fell, the temperature dropped steeply. A cold wind rattled against the windowpanes. Heavy clouds blocked the full moon and threatened us with snow. I slipped into bed next to Meri and pulled the comforter up around my ears. I snuggled against her as best as my stomach would let me and put an arm around her waist. She didn't move. I raised my head to look at her.

"Are you asleep?" I asked.

"No."

"What's wrong, then? Are you mad at me?"

"A little," she said without moving.

"Why?"

"You were supposed to go shopping with me tomorrow, not your mother."

I pulled away from her a bit. "You hate shopping, Meri. Besides, it was very nice of my mother to ask. We've never been shopping together. First steps and all that."

"I don't hate shopping," she said. "I just hate the people you run into while you're shopping. I thought we could buy some baby things while we were out, you know, to start putting together a nursery or something."

"We can still do that, Meri. You just tell me what to get and we'll get right to work on it as soon as I get home."

She turned over. She was scowling pretty fiercely. "That's not the point, Bea. It was something that we were going to do together. We're supposed to be a family, remember? You and me and the baby."

"And sometimes Taylor."

"Don't push it, Biker Babe. I'm already mad at you."

"Meri, come on. You can't keep getting mad every time someone takes a little of my time."

She crossed her arms. "Just watch me."

I rolled my eyes at her, but she was too busy glowering to notice. "Okay then, how about if we compromise a little. I'll go clothes shopping with my mother tomorrow, you and I can go baby shopping on Saturday, and we won't invite Taylor over for Christmas dinner."

"That's still not the point, and besides, we're having dinner at Aunt Beatrice's and there's no way on God's green earth that you'll convince her not to invite golden boy Taylor."

"Then you're going to have to tell me what the point of all this is, because I don't have a clue what you're upset about."

Meri's face crumpled and her eyes squeezed shut. She turned her back to me and put the pillow over her head. "You don't need me anymore," she said with a muffled sob.

"Where did that come from?"

She didn't answer. I lifted the pillow and peeked under it at her. She pulled it down. I grabbed it, tore it out of her hands and threw it on the floor. She grabbed my pillow and put it over her head, and I threw that one on the floor too. "Talk to me, Meri. Don't hide."

Meri rolled over again to glare at me. "This morning you needed me to take you shopping, and now you don't." She kept glaring, lips pressed tight together, her chin trembling slightly.

"This is about money? I don't believe it." Of all the things we could be arguing about, money would have been the very last thing on my list.

"This is about you needing me to help you keep a roof over your head."

"Are you saying that you think I've been staying here only because I need you to provide for me?" I asked, anger creeping into my voice.

"No, that's not what I'm saying." Her glare flickered a little. "Well, maybe it's sort of what I'm saying. Before today, your options were limited. Now you have choices."

"And you think that with all my new choices I'll un-choose you?"

She lay still, her hands clutching at the comforter. "Yes," she said softly. "The money changes everything. You can go live wherever you want to now." She drew the cover up and tucked it under her chin. "You can go live in some fancy apartment in some big city and eat artichoke hearts and asparagus salad until your skin turns green. You can buy a big house somewhere a lot more fashionable than here with neighbors who know not to wash their feet in the bidet."

I laughed because I couldn't help it. "When did you ever wash your feet in a bidet?"

"I'm not telling, and that's still not the point!"

"What's the point, Meri?"

She pulled the covers over her head. "The point is that now you can buy a new motorcycle," she said from underneath the blankets.

"Meri, you're a big doofus."

"I am not."

"You are, too," I said, pulling the comforter down and tucking it back under her chin. "First of all, motorcycles don't come with child safety seats, and second, while I appreciate everything you've done for me from Band-Aiding my head to pulling me out of the barn, I don't love you for it."

Her eyes went wide and surprised. "You don't?"

"No," I said, putting my hand to her cheek. "I don't love you for the things you've done. I love you for who you are, and no amount of money is going to change that."

Meri shook her head sharply and my hand fell away from her face. "I know you think that's true, Bea, but you're being naive. Money does change things."

I rolled over and frowned at the ceiling. "There's one thing that I know is going to change."

"What?"

"You're going to have to learn to trust me as much as I've had to learn to trust you. And if you can't, well, maybe that should tell us something." I turned my back to her and pulled the comforter around my ears. My head felt funny resting against the mattress, but I wasn't about to ask her to pick up my pillow for me.

I felt the bed move as she reached to shut off the light. She settled down, leaving her own pillow on the floor, too. She lay very still behind me. I listened to her breathe, waiting for it to smooth out as she drifted off to sleep, but it didn't. She sighed heavily, blowing out a long, low whistle. She rolled over and pressed herself against my back. Her arm slipped around my waist, and she kissed my shoulder with a soft brush of her lips.

"I'm sorry, Bea," she said quietly, her words whispering across my skin. "I'm scared. I'm scared of so many things that I don't know what to be scared of first. You're so beautiful that sometimes I have a hard time understanding what someone like you would want with someone like me." She touched her lips to the back of my neck. "It wasn't so bad when your only options were to stay here or to run. But that's all changed now. I don't have anything to offer you that you can't get better and cheaper somewhere else."

I turned in her arms and faced her. The moon shone in through the window throwing soft shadows across her face. She blew sharply against my chin. Toothpaste and mouthwash, mint and cinnamon. I cradled her face in my hands. "There's not another Meri Donovan to be found anywhere else in this world for any amount of money in any place other than where I am right now." She blinked rapidly, and I leaned in to kiss her fluttering lashes. "And where else would I ever find another horse like Sergeant?"

"Do you still want to marry me?" she asked. "You don't have to, you know."

I shifted a little to look at her. "I still want to if you don't mind waiting until after the baby is born."

"Why do you want to wait?" she asked, her fingers tracing a soft tingly line across my collarbone.

"Well, who ever heard of a maternity wedding gown?"

She grinned. "I'm sure there's got to be some out there, but who says you get to wear the dress? I'm shorter, I should get to wear the dress and you should have to wear a tux."

I raised an eyebrow at her. "A maternity tuxedo? I think not. You have broader shoulders than I do. You should wear the tux."

"I have a short torso," she said shaking her head. "I would look stupid in a cummerbund."

"I don't think they even make cummerbunds big enough to fit me. Besides, I'd feel ridiculous in a bow tie. How about if we both wear a dress?"

She pressed her hand flat against my chest, her palm dipping between my breasts. "You would look wonderful even in a bathrobe."

"Not anymore, I don't." I moved her hand down to the bulge of my stomach.

She rubbed her hand in circles over my belly, and things

started fluttering inside. "Bea, so many things are changing, and if you think about it, it really hasn't been that long."

"What are you asking me, Meri?"

She leaned in closer to me. "Are you sure? I mean, really sure? People change, you know. You might not like me five years from now."

Her breath came warmly against my lips. I touched her mouth with my fingers and lifted my head to kiss her. My hands moved down her neck and over her breasts. Her nipples tightened under my palms.

"Here's something that will never change," I said, feeling the hard nub of her sliding between my fingers.

She laughed in a short, choked gasp and leaned in hard against my hands. "Touch me," she said in a whisper.

And I did.

Christmas Day dawned with the snow still falling. Fat snowflakes fell silently to the ground, covering and layering, evening things out and smoothing them down, turning the harsh dead browns of winter into soft hills of gray-white. I stood with my nose pressed against the windowpane, exhaling frost onto the glass. It was the first time I'd ever seen a white covered Christmas outside of postcards and old reruns of holiday movies. It was even more amazing when it wasn't in grainy black and white.

I watched Meri from the kitchen window making the long, slow trek to the west side of the pasture to the old sheep shed where we were keeping Sergeant housed until his new barn could be built. He'd been indignant, at first, to be sleeping in a place that still smelled like sheep, but now he didn't seem to want to come out. Meri opened his pasture door and he walked out into the snow, made a great big circle and went right back inside. I guess he'd seen enough snow in his life not to get excited over it. I was thrilled right down to my toes. I could hardly contain myself as I bustled around the kitchen.

I heard Meri stomping her boots against the porch before the kitchen door opened with a whirl of cold and wet. She stepped inside, and immediately the snowflakes in her hair started melting into crystal drops.

I frowned at her poor ragged head. "Honestly, Meri, why didn't you wear a hat?" I asked with my hands on my hips, waving my dishtowel at her, the very picture of a scolding housewife. I tried hard not to crack a smile. "You only have two inches of hair. That's not enough to keep your head warm. If you don't cover up, you'll catch your death of cold and then where would I be?"

She hunched her shoulders inside her jacket and stomped heavily across the kitchen floor. Her face was scowling, but her eyes were laughing at me. "Leave me alone, woman. And where's my breakfast?" she growled and hitched at her pants. Her lips twitched.

We both started snickering. "That wasn't very convincing."

She leaned over and kissed my cheek with winter cold lips. "Sorry. I guess I didn't have the right role models." She rubbed her hand over her head slicking her hair against her scalp. "The snow does sting a little when it hits my bald spot."

"You do have a hat, don't you?"

"Sure do. There are four or five of them in the hall closet."

I watched a drop of snow melt from the end of a spike of hair and drip onto her shoulder. "Can I borrow one?"

"You know you don't have to ask," Meri said as she slipped her coat off and hung it over the back of a kitchen chair. She looked at me suspiciously. "Why do you need one?"

"I want to go outside and make a snowman," I answered with a grin. "We should make it in the pasture, so Sergeant can come out and eat the carrot if he wants to."

Meri shook her head as she went to pour herself a cup of coffee. "He'd be just as likely to kick the whole thing into next week as eat the nose off it." She added cream and sugar and stirred. "And what's this 'we' stuff?"

"Don't you want to build a snowman?"

182

She shrugged and blew into her cup. "I've built them before," she said and took a sip.

"Well, there you have it. I need your expertise."

"It's not complicated, Bea. The big ball goes on the bottom, medium one in the middle, little one on top."

I laid a hand on my stomach and gave her my best puppy dog eyes. "And you're going to make me lift all that snow by myself?"

Meri snorted into her coffee. "Can it wait until after breakfast?"

I grinned and crossed the kitchen to kiss her on the cheek. "You always say the most charming things."

"Shoot. If I were so charming, I'd convince you to go back to bed instead of agreeing to go outside and play in the snow," she said with a hopeful glance.

"How about a compromise? Snow right now and we'll go to bed early tonight."

She shook her head. "That's no good. You know Aunt Beatrice is going to stuff us tighter than the turkey. We'll come right home and fall asleep." She tilted her head. "How about if we stay in bed all day tomorrow?"

There was a flutter in my belly at the thought of a whole day of languid nakedness and Meri's skillful hands. "That sounds like a reasonable compromise," I said as calmly as I could.

Meri grinned. I wasn't fooling her one bit. The phone rang. Meri set her coffee on the counter and reached to answer it.

"Good morning, Auntie. A Merry Christmas to you, too." I heard her say as I turned to rummage through the refrigerator. I took out the eggs and a block of sharp cheddar thinking that I could make a couple of omelets that Meri probably wouldn't hate too much. I shot her a glance over my shoulder while I dug through the vegetable drawer for the green peppers and onions. Her back was turned, but there was an all-too-familiar set to her shoulders.

"All right," she said into the phone a little ungraciously. "What time?"

I closed the refrigerator door and leaned against it to wait for the bad news. No doubt, Aunt Beatrice had something she wanted us to do that I probably wouldn't like very much, like come early and bring an extra dish, or maybe she wanted Meri and me to sit at the children's table. Whatever it was, Meri had already committed us with her "all right."

Meri hung up the phone, turned and gave me a look.

"Hey, now," I said holding up a hand, "whatever it is, I didn't put her up to it, so don't go looking at me like that."

Meri still looked sullen. "Aunt Beatrice says that she accidentally invited too many people to fit into her dining room."

I took that to mean we were being banished to the children's table. I set the onion down on the counter with a thunk. "I guess it would be too much to hope that she's uninvited us."

Meri shook her head. "She wants us to have Christmas dinner over here."

"What? There's no way that can happen. We don't have enough food here to feed twenty people."

"It's now thirty people, not including all the children."

"Good god, Meri, what's she thinking? We don't have that much room either."

Meri's shoulders slumped. "We do if we open the connecting doors between the dinning room and the parlor. We can put the kids at tables in the den."

"Even if. We still don't have time to put a dinner together. It's Christmas. All the stores are closed."

"She said that everybody would bring a little something. She's got two turkeys and a ham going now."

"And you've already told her that we would."

"She seemed pretty set on it."

"Crap." I turned back toward the kitchen counter and selected a knife, bigger than necessary, to chop the onion. "I really wanted to build the snowman before we had to go to dinner. Now we have to clean."

"No, we don't." Meri grabbed a bowl from the cupboard and cracked an egg against the side. "Auntie is sending over an advance scouting party to do whatever cleaning and setting up that needs to be done. We don't have to do a thing but let them in."

My knife froze in mid-chop. "Then what are you so unhappy about?"

Meri cracked an egg hard enough so that half of it dribbled onto the counter. "She invited forty people, but some of them won't come if it's being held over here."

"Why not?"

"Who knows?" she said, reaching for another egg. "Maybe they're afraid that we'll bump noses under the mistletoe. God forbid that I should kiss you in front of the children. As if anybody ever kisses anybody in front of the children." She put the egg back into the carton, turned to me and laid a hand on my stomach, now decently covered in a fluffy pleated sweater. "Maybe they're afraid of the questions this will raise."

"Wouldn't they ask the same questions over at Aunt Beatrice's house?"

"Not in a million years. They'd be too busy trying to sit still and not scuff the furniture."

I set the knife down and put my hands over hers. "What I hear you saying is that in their natural environment these kids aren't the 'be seen and not heard' type."

She smiled wryly. "No, indeed they're not." She wiggled her fingers under mine. "They're the, '*Hey, aren't you the lady with the cool motorcycle-ain't you the one who set the barn on fire-how'd you get that scar on your head-why are you pregnant and not married?*' type."

"Precocious little things, aren't they?"

"That's one word for it."

"Okay," I said, taking a breath, "so when are they coming?"

"The cooking and cleaning party should arrive at one. The dinner is still on for four."

"It's only nine now," I said, giving her my wiggly eyebrow

185

look.

"What about it?" she asked, squinting her eyes at me.

"You know what we have time for?"

"Sex?" she said hopefully.

"Snow."

She pulled a face and turned back to the eggs. "Some present that is, you dragging me out into the snow on Christmas morning."

"You're the one who didn't want to do presents, remember? You said birthdays are for presents and Christmas is for family?"

"Did I say that?"

"You most certainly did."

She sighed and whipped a fork around in the eggs fast enough to raise a froth. "Fine. Snow. But after breakfast, okay?"

"Immediately after. Do we have any carrots?"

"Bottom drawer on the right." Meri poured the eggs into a pan and sprinkled the onions on top. "See if there are any radishes in there. We can use those for eyes."

I giggled and headed for the refrigerator.

Snow is much heavier than it looks. It caught me by surprise as we rolled the three circles around in the pasture. It looked so light and fluffy coming down, all lace filigree and intricate patterns. It seemed to me that it should be as light as a spider's web, but Meri reminded me that, in the end, snow is just frozen water, and water can be awfully heavy, especially when you have to carry buckets and buckets of it all the way across the pasture to fill Sergeant's trough. I asked her how many snowflakes did she think it took to build a snowman, but Meri couldn't find a ruler small enough to measure a single snowflake, and besides, they kept falling in all different sizes. I knew there had to be a better way to go about it, but we still had a lot of fun catching snowflakes and drawing zeros in the snow.

We used a carrot for the nose, of course, and radishes for the eyes, apple slices for the mouth just to keep everything horse edible, though Sergeant didn't care much for apples anymore. Meri put a John Deere cap on the snowman's head and tucked an ugly plaid scarf under its chin that almost matched the plaid of the coat I was wearing. I wanted to give the snowman two faces. I thought it would be more fun for Sergeant that way, who stood peering at us through the open door of the sheep pen, but Meri thought it would be too creepy to look at, and anyway, it might give him a bellyache to eat too many radishes. His stomach was still pretty sensitive.

I was busy adjusting the stick arms when something splat against the side of my head. Something very cold and very wet. I turned and saw Meri stoop to scoop up another handful of snow.

"Oh, no you don't," I yelled and ducked behind the snowman.

A snowball whizzed over my head. I knelt to grab my own handful of snow when something hit me in the stomach. I looked down at myself. A snowball splat against my shoulder, but I didn't pay any attention to it.

"What is it, Bea?" Meri called out to me.

I didn't answer. I put both hands on my stomach and it hit me again, harder this time. From the inside.

"Oh, god," I said softly, sitting in the snow.

Meri skidded to a stop beside me. She knelt and slid her arms around my shoulders. "Bea, what is it? What's wrong? What hurts?"

I looked into her confusion and concern, into her pale blue eyes that today matched the color of the sky behind her, and the enormity of what we had undertaken hit me, like a little foot against my rib cage. Right at that moment, that little foot stopped being a vague concept. It was not teddy bear wallpaper and tiny pairs of socks, not fuzzy pink blankets and pastel jumpers, not the intellectual ponderings of mother-daughter relationships. That little foot was not just a means to an end.

Meri and I were going to have a baby. My heart swelled in a way that I'd never felt before. I leaned into Meri and felt nothing but love.

"Meri, take off your glove and give me your hand."

She still looked confused, but she gave me her hand and I slid it underneath my coat. Her palm lay flat and cold against my belly. The baby kicked again, and Meri's eyes went wide. She rubbed her hands over my stomach and her face broke into a grin. "She wants to come out and play, too."

I laughed and then I cried as I pulled her head down to me. She kissed me hard, and I got lost in the press of her lips, the caress of her hand, the soft tickle of her hair as it slid through my fingers.

"What the hell do you two think you're doing?" A deep voice boomed from across the pasture.

Meri lifted her head slowly, reluctantly. Taylor climbed over the fence and came stomping through the snow. He stood over us, the hands on his hips balled into tight angry fists.

"Bea, why are you sitting in the snow? Meri, why are you letting her? Christ on a crutch, don't you know that baby's naked in there? It's not wearing a sweater and earmuffs."

I laughed at him and his scowl deepened. "Taylor, kneel down here and give me your hand."

"What?" He looked at me like I had gone crazier than one of his betsey bugs.

"Come here and give me your hand," I repeated slowly.

Meri tensed and frowned, but she didn't say anything. I kissed her cheek and the frown softened. Taylor knelt and gave me his hand. I pulled off his glove and started to put his hand underneath my coat. He snatched his hand away and shot Meri a wide-eyed frightened look.

Meri gave an exasperated little sigh. "Just do it, Taylor."

Taylor gave me his hand back and I put it under my coat right next to Meri's. I smiled at him.

"What am I doing this for?" he asked, confused and a little

embarrassed.

"Just wait," I said.

The baby kicked again. Taylor jerked. "What was that? Was that the baby? Is that normal? Is everything all right? Should I call a doctor?"

Meri snorted. "You haven't read a single damn book, have you? And you call yourself a father."

My smile broke into a grin. "It's a good thing, Taylor. She's just moving around in there."

"Really?" Taylor's face was a mix of wonder and disbelief and then the baby shifted in a long slow roll underneath all of our hands. Taylor pulled his hand away from me, looked at it with glittering eyes and pressed it to his chest. He leaned down suddenly and swept me into a hug, his stubbly face scratching against my neck.

Meri jerked back with her eyes blazing. "Hey . . ." she started to say.

"Oh, shut up," Taylor said and wrapped his other arm around her. He pulled the three of us tight in together. Meri stayed stiff and rigid against his arm until I reached down and rubbed her butt. She gave me a frustrated growl and slipped her arm around my waist.

Horns blared from the driveway. We broke apart, Taylor wiping his nose and looking a little chagrined. A line of cars crunched over the drive beeping and flashing their headlights. They pulled up to the house and about a dozen people spilled out with buckets and mops, brooms and dustpans, bottles and rags. They shouted and hollered at us, waving and laughing. Meri laughed too and shook her head. "I guess that's the cleaning crew."

"And the cooking crew, too," I said, pointing to the line of tinfoil-covered dishes and armloads of grocery bags ducking into the kitchen. Taylor stood and pulled us both to our feet. He looked at Meri and me with a huge lopsided grin spread across his face.

"Merry Christmas to all," he said still holding our hands, "and

189

especially to me."

"Taylor, you're such an ass," Meri said with the barest hint of a smile.

Turkey and dressing, cranberry sauce and green been casserole, sweet potato pie, crisply chilled apple wine, bright lights and laughter. I'd never had a Christmas dinner like this. It was a madhouse. It was mayhem. It was a marvel. I was deeply in love with everyone there.

Meri was radiant with her wine-blushed cheeks and the fuzzy reindeer horns someone brought her as a gift. Taylor seemed larger than life when he stood to carve the ham in his red Santa hat, his eyes bright and shining. Aunt Bea sat at the head of the table as if it were her proper place in the world. My mother sat at her right hand, looking small in her chair but wide-eyed with wonder. The children ran and shouted, their mothers scolding half-heartedly, as plates were passed and glasses filled and filled again.

"Oh no, we're out of rolls," said the cousin on my left, a red haired and freckled girl sitting in an awkward stage of too old to be a child but still too young to be an adult. She rose a little in her chair. "Heya, Andy, you guys got some rolls in there?" she yelled into the den.

"Incoming!" was the answer.

A roll flew through the air in a graceful arc and landed with a splat in a bowl of mashed potatoes.

"Andrew Duncan, you stop throwing food around in there, ya hear?" shouted a voice from the end of the table. Another voice, loud and proud, started to tell a story about a legendary food fight in the high school cafeteria as other voices chimed in with the details of hamburger Frisbees and flying french fries. I was laughing so hard that I almost missed hearing the doorbell ring. At the end of the table, I saw Meri lean over toward Aunt Beatrice. Auntie shrugged. Meri wiped her lips and got up from the table.

"Excuse me, honey, could you pass the green beans?" asked a cousin sitting across the table from me. She was a large woman with a razor sharp wit, sitting next to her small skinny husband who had spent the afternoon saying the craziest things in a deadpan monotone. I had come to like them both very much. I watched her serve a tiny portion of green beans to him and pile a huge mound onto her own plate while she dissected, in weighty philosophical tones, the fallacies of the Jack Sprat story. I was tittering to myself, when I felt a hand on my shoulder. I looked up into Meri's pale face.

"What is it?" I asked, reaching for her hand.

"The door," she said. "It's for you." I saw her eyes dart over to my mother, who was watching us out of the corner of her eye.

I folded my napkin and Meri helped me out of the chair.

"Who is it?" I asked, but I already knew.

"Your father's on the porch."

On my porch where he had no right to be. And on Christmas Day. I felt a slow burning anger kindle in the place where my fear used to lie. I tossed my napkin onto my chair. "Is he with an army of lawyers or just a gaggle of butt kissers?"

Meri shook her head. "He's alone."

My anger flittered and snuffed out. "What do you mean alone?"

"Alone as in nobody is with him. He's by himself."

"Not even Weasel?"

She shook her head again. "Do you want me to tell him to go away?"

I expected to see the cold deadness take over her eyes, but it never came. Only pity and unease drifted across her face.

"No," I said, gripping her hand. "Thank you, Meri. I'll go tell him myself."

She squeezed my hand back and let it go. I went to the door.

I found my father sitting on the porch swing, still and waiting. He looked terrible, thin and haggard and old. Really old. Older

191

than Methuselah, Meri would say. His coat hung limp across the hunch of his shoulders, his slacks were uncreased, his steel-gray hair was wild and natty. A week's worth of beard stuck like wet ashes against his chin. It shocked me a little. I had always thought of my father as eternal and unchanging. Here was one more thing I would have to unlearn.

He had two small wrapped packages in his hands. Silver foiled paper, red and green ribbons. I stepped onto the front porch and stood looking down at him for the first time that I could ever remember. He looked up at me with an expression that was strange and haunted. His eyes roamed over my scar and then dropped to my stomach. He frowned suddenly and looked at his feet. He'd never done that before in his life. I watched his Adam's apple bob as he swallowed.

"It's Christmas," he said. His blood and thunder voice sounded cracked and broken.

I took a deep breath. "Yes, it is."

He nodded his head toward the front door. "Sounds like quite a bash."

I shrugged. "It's Christmas."

"Yes, it is," he said softy. He didn't say anything else, and it didn't seem like he was going to.

I glanced over my shoulder at the front door and wished that I were on the other side. "The party," I said, for the sake of saying something, "it's a tradition around here. The whole extended family gets together on Christmas. Saves bouncing around from house to house. It's because of the snow, I think, and the mountains. Traveling around too much can be dangerous this time of year, so . . ." I shut my mouth when I realized that I was rambling.

"Seems like a good idea," he said, looking at the mountains where the white snow capped the dark, sleepy trees.

"Yes, I guess it does."

He gestured with one of the gifts that he held in his hands. "I brought you something. For you and . . ." He waved it at the door.

"Meri. Her name is Meri."

"I brought something for you and Meri," he said very precisely as if saying her name made his lips uncomfortable. Maybe it did.

"Because it's Christmas?" I asked with a light touch of sarcasm.

"Because you're my daughter." A spark of anger flared in his eyes and then died leaving behind only an empty kind of sadness. "You're my daughter," he repeated. "Somewhere along the way, I think I forgot that."

I don't think he ever knew it in the first place, but if he was starting to get it now, then I was willing to let it go.

He raised the second box. "I brought something for your mother, too. I heard she was here or that you probably knew where to find her."

There was no body language to contradict his words, no hidden agenda written in the curl of his lip, only the tired bend of his back, the sad squint of his eyes. "She's here, but I don't think she wants to see you."

He nodded and held both gifts out to me. "Would you give it to her? It's not much, just a little something."

"Sure," I said and took the boxes from him. "Thank you."

He set his empty hands on his knees. "That's all I came for." He stood. "I'll let you get back to your party." He brushed past me, stepped carefully down the porch stairs and started down the path toward the driveway and the long line of cars parked there. The last car in the line was a deep blue Cadillac with thirty-day tags. Quite a modest car for him, considering, and I didn't even know my father knew how to drive. There were probably a lot of things that I didn't know about my father. I wondered if any of them were good things.

"Dad?"

He turned around with a strange mix of emotions on his face.

I jerked my chin toward the front door. "Why don't you come in? We'll put you at a different table than mom."

He smiled, sad and radiant all at the same time. "Thank you, Collier," he said, but he shook his head. "I appreciate it, but I don't think it would be a good idea. Your mother . . ." His eyes cut to the trees, pinched and squinting. "I haven't treated her very well."

"No, you haven't."

Anger flashed again and then died. He looked back at me. "Or you either."

"Or me either."

"I'm going to try to change that."

I didn't know what to say. It was almost an apology, but it wasn't quite. "It'll take some time," I finally said to him a little doubtfully.

He put his hands in his pockets. It made his shoulders slump even more. "Just so you know, in case people come asking, I resigned my seat yesterday. It's probably not in the papers yet with the holidays here."

I was speechless. His seat in the senate was the one thing he coveted more than anything else. It was the one thing he prized more than money, more than fame, more than family. It had allowed him to be the power behind the president for more years than I could remember. It had brought the presidency nearly within his grasp. I couldn't imagine him giving that up. Not even the hope of it. I wondered how bad things had really gotten for him. Aunt Beatrice and three fourths of the senate body would be beside themselves with joy, but right then and there, it only made me sad.

"So, now you'll have time."

"I'm going to try to spend it a little more wisely."

I smiled at him as best I could. "That sounds like a good plan."

He nodded his head at me and turned. He walked past the line of cars, got into his Cadillac and backed it down the drive. It

194

turned onto the road. There was a brief flash from his taillights, and then he was gone.

The front door opened behind me and my mother stepped onto the porch.

"Did you hear any of that?" I asked.

She nodded. "I heard most of it. The door wasn't shut all the way."

"He brought you something." I held out the gift with the green ribbons.

She shook her head. "Will you keep it for me? I'm not sure I want it just yet."

"Sure." The wind blew, and I shivered a little. "We'd better go inside. It's cold out here, and I'm sure Meri's worried."

"Frantic," she said with a smile.

I laughed, a sad little laugh, and shook my head. I turned toward the door, but my mother laid a hand on my arm. "Collier." She stopped herself. "Bea, don't let me stand in the way of you making peace with your father if you can. I know it sounds crazy right now, but he does love you in his own way."

In the driveway I could see the tracks in the snow where the Cadillac had been. "His own way is capricious and cruel. I don't believe that it ever was love." I felt the weight of the packages in my hand. "But that doesn't mean it never will be."

I turned back toward the house. Meri was looking out the parlor window, her fuzzy reindeer horns still on her head. Taylor was hovering over her shoulder with his Santa hat drooping. I could see Meri's funny eyes, dark gray today against the blue of her sweater, and it made me laugh, a real laugh, a belly shaking, rib cracking, heart-healing laugh just because I loved her so much.

Our future was rosy and bright. We had family. We had friends. We had each other. And if there were bad things hiding just around the corner, I knew, now, that we had the strength and the resolve to see them through.

Meri grinned at me with a nod of understanding and blew

me a kiss. The curtain fell into place as I wiped at my eyes with a corner of my sleeve. My mother smiled and gave my arm a pat.

"Let's go inside," she said and we headed back into the warmth and bright lights.

Publications from

BELLA BOOKS, INC.

The best in contemporary lesbian fiction
P.O. Box 10543, Tallahassee, FL 32302
Phone: 800-729-4992
www.bellabooks.com

WITHOUT WARNING: Book one in the Shaken series by KG MacGregor. *Without Warning* is the story of their courageous journey through adversity, and their promise of steadfast love.
978-1-59493-120-8 $13.95

THE CANDIDATE by Tracey Richardson. Presidential candidate Jane Kincaid had always expected the road to the White House would exact a high personal toll. She just never knew how high until forced to choose between her heart and her political destiny.
978-1-59493-133-8 $13.95

TALL IN THE SADDLE by Karin Kallmaker, Barbara Johnson, Therese Szymanski and Julia Watts. The playful quartet that penned the acclaimed *Once Upon A Dyke* and *Stake Through the Heart* are back and now turning to the Wild (and Very Hot) West to bring you another collection of erotically charged, action-packed, tales.
978-1-59493-106-2 $15.95

IN THE NAME OF THE FATHER by Gerri Hill. In this highly anticipated sequel to *Hunter's Way*, Dallas homicide detectives Tori Hunter and Samantha Kennedy investigate the murder of a Catholic priest who is found naked and strangled to death.
978-1-59493-108-6 $13.95

IT'S ALL SMOKE AND MIRRORS: The First Chronicles of Shawn Donnelly by Therese Szymanski. Join Therese Szymanski as she takes a walk on the sillier side of the gritty crime-scene detective novel and introduces readers to her newest alternate personality—Shawn Donnelly.
978-1-59493-117-8 $13.95

THE ROAD HOME by Frankie J. Jones. As Lynn finds herself in one adventure after another, she discovers that true wealth may have very little to do with money after all.
978-1-59493-110-9 $13.95

IN DEEP WATERS: CRUISING THE SEAS by Karin Kallmaker and Radclyffe. Book passage on a deliciously sensual Mediterranean cruise with tour guides Radclyffe and Karin Kallmaker.
978-1-59493-111-6 $15.95

ALL THAT GLITTERS by Peggy J. Herring. Life is good for retired Army colonel Marcel Robicheaux. Marcel is unprepared for the turn her life will take. She soon finds herself in the pursuit of a lifetime—searching for her missing mother and lover.
978-1-59493-107-9 $13.95

OUT OF LOVE by KG MacGregor. For Carmen Delallo and Judith O'Shea, falling in love proves to be the easy part.
978-1-59493-105-5 $13.95

BORDERLINE by Terri Breneman. Assistant prosecuting attorney Toni Barston returns in the sequel to *Anticipation*.
978-1-59493-99-7 $13.95

PAST REMEMBERING by Lyn Denison. What would it take to melt Peri's cool exterior? Any involvement on Asha's part would be simply asking for trouble and heartache . . . wouldn't it?   978-1-59493-103-1 $13.95

ASPEN'S EMBERS by Diane Tremain Braund. Will Aspen choose the woman she loves. . . or the forest she hopes to preserve.   978-1-59493-102-4 $14.95

THE COTTAGE by Gerri Hill. *The Cottage* is the heartbreaking story of two women who meet by chance . . . or did they? A love so destined it couldn't be denied . . . stolen moments to be cherished forever.   978-1-59493-096-6 $13.95

FANTASY: Untrue Stories of Lesbian Passion edited by Barbara Johnson and Therese Szymanski. Lie back and let Bella's bad girls take you on an erotic journey through the greatest bedtime stories never told.   978-1-59493-101-7 $15.95

SISTERS' FLIGHT by Jeanne G'Fellers. *Sisters' Flight* is the highly anticipated sequel to *No Sister of Mine* and *Sister Lost, Sister Found*.   978-1-59493-116-1 $13.95

BRAGGIN' RIGHTS by Kenna White. Taylor Fleming is a thirty-six-year-old Texas rancher who covets her independence. She finds her cowgirl independence tested by neighboring rancher Jen Holland.   978-1-59493-095-9 $13.95

BRILLIANT by Ann Roberts. Respected sociology professor, Diane Cole finds her views on love challenged by her own heart, as she fights the attraction she feels for a woman half her age.   978-1-59493-115-4 $13.95

THE EDUCATION OF ELLIE by Jackie Calhoun. When Ellie sees her childhood friend for the first time in thirty years she is tempted to resume their long lost friendship. But with the years come a lot of baggage and the two women struggle with who they are now while fighting the painful memories of their first parting. Will they be able to move past their history to start again?   978-1-59493-092-8 $13.95

DATE NIGHT CLUB by Saxon Bennett. *Date Night Club* is a dark romantic comedy about the pitfalls of dating in your thirties . . .   978-1-59493-094-2 $13.95

PLEASE FORGIVE ME by Megan Carter. Laurel Becker is on the verge of losing the two most important things in her life—her current lover, Elaine Alexander, and the Lavender Page bookstore. Will Elaine and Laurel manage to work through their misunderstandings and rebuild their life together?   978-1-59493-091-1 $13.95

WHISKEY AND OAK LEAVES by Jaime Clevenger. Meg meets June, a single woman running a horse ranch in the California Sierra foothills. The two become quick friends and it isn't long before Meg is looking for more than just a friendship. But June has no interest in developing a deeper relationship with Meg. She is, after all, not the least bit interested in women . . . or is she? Neither of these two women is prepared for what lies ahead . . .   978-1-59493-093-5 $13.95

SUMTER POINT by KG MacGregor. As Audie surrenders her heart to Beth, she begins to distance herself from the reckless habits of her youth. Just as they're ready to meet in the middle, their future is thrown into doubt by a duty Beth can't ignore. It all comes to a head on the river at Sumter Point.   978-1-59493-089-8 $13.95

THE TARGET by Gerri Hill. Sara Michaels is the daughter of a prominent senator who has been receiving death threats against his family. In an effort to protect Sara, the FBI recruits homicide detective Jaime Hutchinson to secretly provide the protection they are so certain Sara will need. Will Sara finally figure out who is behind the death threats? And will Jaime realize the truth—and be able to save Sara before it's too late?
                                                978-1-59493-082-9 $13.95